D1246681

SAINT ELIZABETH'S THREE CROWNS

SAINT ELIZABETH'S THREE CROWNS

Written by Blanche Jennings Thompson
Illustrated by Lili Rethi

IGNATIUS PRESS   SAN FRANCISCO

Published by Farrar, Straus and Cudahy, Inc.
(now Farrar, Straus, Giroux, Inc.)
A Vision Book
With ecclesiastical approval
Reprinted with permission

Cover art by Christopher J. Pelicano
Cover design by Riz Boncan Marsella

Published by Ignatius Press, San Francisco, 1996
ISBN 978-0-89870-596-6
Library of Congress catalogue number 96–83642
Printed in the United States of America ⬭

Manufactured by Thomson-Shore, Dexter, MI (USA); RMA572LS523, February 2011

CONTENTS

I

THE TINY PRINCESS

"WHAT DO YOU THINK Princess Elizabeth will look like?"

"How old is she, Dame Bertha?"

"Is King Andrew very rich?"

Dame Bertha of Bendeleiben shook her head. She was a plump lady, a countess who lived in the Wartburg Castle in Thuringia, a part of Germany. She was handsome and richly dressed, but right now she was not any too comfortable. She and her companions were bumping along a rough road in a great gilded coach drawn by six white horses decorated with jeweled harness and crimson plumes.

Before the coach and beside it, stalwart Thuringian knights rode, two by two, on spirited steeds. A second gilded coach followed, along with a train of servants in wagons and on horseback. The early spring green of fields and pastures made a background for the brilliant color of banners and pennons. The velvet cloaks of the knights, the jeweled trappings of the horses, and the gold of the coaches rivaled the sun itself.

"Let me get myself well settled," said Dame Bertha, "and I will tell you what I know."

The countess and her companions, two pretty, fair-haired young women named Ilse and Odilia, arranged themselves as comfortably as possible, pulling the fur robes up closely, for it was still chilly, and placing velvet cushions back of their heads and shoulders. They had a very long journey ahead of them, for they were on their way to the court of King Andrew of Hungary.

These Thuringian nobles were traveling in the year 1211, in the period now known as the Middle Ages. It was an exciting and colorful period, in which kings and princes ruled over small states and made continual war upon each other. It was also a time of great religious fervor, when the ruling classes believed that they were serving God with all their hearts. At the same time, some thought nothing of murder and pillage, and they enslaved and ill-treated their fellowmen.

Early in this period of strange contrasts and contradictions, Princess Elizabeth of Hungary was born. It was because of her that the golden coaches were rumbling along the muddy road on their way to the Pressburg Castle.

"Now, Dame Bertha, tell us about Elizabeth", said Ilse eagerly. She and Odilia were greatly envied by the other ladies of the Thuringian court because they had been chosen to go with Dame Bertha. They intended to bring back from Hungary the little girl who was to marry, when she was old enough, Louis, the son of Landgrave Hermann, ruler of Thuringia. Now they wanted to know more about their errand.

"Well," said Dame Bertha, "let us begin at the beginning. You have lived long enough at the Wartburg Castle to know that Landgrave Hermann needs strong allies to help him protect his property. Louis must marry the daughter of some powerful prince."

"Yes, of course," replied Ilse, "but why didn't the landgrave choose a princess of some country nearer to Thuringia?"

"That", answered Dame Bertha, "is a story in itself. You have heard, no doubt, of the poet Klingsohr, who claims to be able to foretell future events by reading the stars. Well, about four years ago, in the year 1207, a number of poets and minstrels were gathered in an inn not far from the Wartburg. They were all out on a balcony gazing up at the stars when Klingsohr made a mysterious announcement. He said that on that night a daughter had been born to the king of Hungary and that she would marry the son of Landgrave Hermann. He said, too, that the child would be holy and that she would bring great honor to her family and country and be glorified by the whole Christian Church."

When Dame Bertha saw the startled look in the eyes of Ilse and Odilia, she regretted having told the story.

"Do not mention this tale at court," she said quickly, "especially to Landgravine Sophie. It is only a story, and she does not like to have it repeated. The Princess Elizabeth was actually born that night, but how could Klingsohr foretell that she would be holy? You must realize that such a thing is sheer nonsense."

"But part of the prophecy is true", said Odilia. "The princess *is* going to marry Louis."

"Yes, that part is certainly true", replied Dame Bertha. "When the landgrave heard the prophecy he sent messengers at once to arrange, if possible, for the marriage. King Andrew was delighted, and so was Queen Gertrude. She was a German princess before she married King Andrew, and she has never been really happy in Hungary. She was glad to have her daughter marry the ruler of a German state."

"What is Queen Gertrude like?" asked Ilse.

"I have never seen her, but they say that she is ambitious and ill-tempered and doesn't like to be crossed. I have heard that her fits of rage when things are not to her liking are feared by the whole castle. She likes power and excitement. The Hungarians do not like her because they think she cannot be trusted. They fear that she tells political secrets to German nobles and plots against Hungary."

"And what of King Andrew? Is he like his wife?"

"King Andrew is a very rich and powerful ruler. Minstrels and pilgrims who have stayed at the Wartburg tell wonderful tales of his court. They say that every utensil in the Pressburg Castle is made of gold or silver. The walls are covered with the most costly tapestries, and the jewels of Queen Gertrude are magnificent beyond belief. It is also reported, however, that King Andrew is a weak man and greedy, that he takes the easy way out and does not keep his promises."

"I should not think he would be a very dependable ally for Landgrave Hermann", said Ilse thoughtfully. "Our landgrave is greater and more powerful than King Andrew, is he not?"

"Oh, yes, indeed!" exclaimed Dame Bertha. "Is he not the nephew of the great Emperor Frederick Barbarossa? Our landgrave helped to put young Frederick II, grandson of Barbarossa, on the throne. Emperor Frederick is only seventeen years old, but already they are saying that he will be the greatest emperor the Holy Roman Empire has ever known. Moreover, the Wartburg is a glorious castle. It commands all the roads of Europe. No wonder Landgrave Hermann is so rich and powerful."

"Then, why . . ." began Odilia.

Dame Bertha did not like to be interrupted.

"Landgrave Hermann has many enemies", she went on. "They would like to strip him of his vast fields and forests, his vassals, and his treasures. He has many faithful knights, of course, like Count Meinhardt and Walter of Varila, who are leading this embassy, but he needs strong allies who will send knights and supplies if the Wartburg is attacked or join him in raids on enemy castles."

"But what of the child Elizabeth?" asked Ilse. "Will she be likely to make a good wife for our beloved Louis? The daughter of such parents as you describe hardly seems suitable. I doubt that she would turn out to be holy, in spite of Klingsohr."

"Elizabeth is only four years old. I do not know much about her. It is said that she is small and delicate and has a very cheerful disposition. We are bringing her back to the Wartburg so that she can be educated with Louis and Hermann and Agnes and learn how to behave in a great German castle. She will have much to learn in order to become a worthy mistress of the Wartburg. If Landgravine Sophie finds her unsuitable or unteachable, she will no doubt send her back."

Dame Bertha and her companions lived in a great feudal castle, strongly fortified and defended by armies of knights. Around the castle and close to it for service and protection lived the vassals, the lesser rulers, whose homes were smaller castles, or manors, surrounded by farms and woods. In all these homes hundreds of serfs lived out their lives in virtual slavery, doing the will of their masters under pain of severe punishment or even death.

To the gates of the castle came the beggars and outcasts who lived on the scraps from the rich men's tables. They were grateful for a crust of bread or a coin tossed carelessly to them by a knight or lady. The rich were not intentionally cruel. They really believed that God meant things to be that way.

Ilse and Odilia had never been farther from home than the little village of Eisenach. Now they looked from their golden coach on sights that were strange to them. Along the narrow, crowded road passed pilgrims on foot with staff and begging pouch, headed for the Holy Land. Companies of soldiers raised great clouds of dust, the knights clanking along on their armored horses, the long lines of supply wagons lurching heavily behind, and the foot soldiers plodding wearily in the rear. Once they met a caravan of merchants, and, as they neared a village, they noticed a long religious procession with a bishop at the head. He was followed by a long line of priests and acolytes, swinging their smoking censers.

"What is it, Varila?" called Dame Bertha out the window.

Walter of Varila reined in his horse and rode close to the coach.

"Some knights are going to 'take the cross'. The

bishop is on his way up to that castle on the hill where he will receive the vows of the young knights. Those who take the vow will go to Jerusalem later in the spring to fight the Saracens and save the holy places from the infidels."

Ilse and Odilia watched the procession with interest. They had their favorite knights at the Wartburg. Would they, too, be "taking the cross" and starting the long journey to the holy places? The girls leaned back against the cushions and were silent.

In the great Pressburg Castle in Hungary, where King Andrew and Queen Gertrude kept their court, the little Princess Elizabeth was being made ready to meet the expected guests.

"Stand still, Elizabeth."

Elizabeth was an active child. She did not like to stand still, especially to be dressed in stiff, tight clothes, heavy with rich embroidery, and a golden girdle. She was small for her age, with dark curls and a kind of elfin beauty, and she had a merry smile for everyone.

"This dress is very tight," said Elizabeth, "and how can I run in this big cloak?"

"There will be no more running", said her mother. "If you do not behave as I have taught you, you will not make a good impression on the Thuringian embassy, and they will not take you back with them. Remember, you are to marry Louis, the landgrave's son, and some day you will be landgravine of Thuringia."

"Will Louis play with me?" asked Elizabeth eagerly. "May I take him my golden ball as a present?"

"Your father will send a coach full of presents. Stand *still*, Elizabeth!"

Elizabeth stood still.

Little did Queen Gertrude realize that God was filling the small heart of this child with a great love for him. During her short lifetime she would set an example to the world of Christian charity and humble obedience to God's will.

But all this was yet to come. Right now, the glittering cavalcade of the Thuringian nobles was coming ever closer along the sunny highway. Suddenly, in the towered Pressburg there was a commotion.

"To horse! To horse! Down with the drawbridge!" The shouted orders came from the topmost turret of the castle. Up went the signal flag.

"The Germans are in sight! To horse!"

Into their saddles leaped thirty Hungarian knights, not in the glistening armor of war, but in rich and beautiful garments suited to a peaceful mission. Like the wind they rode on fleet Arabian steeds to meet the Thuringian nobles. Capes of crimson velvet streamed out behind them, and flying eagle plumes made silver clouds against the sky.

Dame Bertha and her companions watched the Hungarian knights as they streamed out over the drawbridge and down the road to meet them. The Germans had come prepared. They had brought rich presents with them, knowing that King Andrew would send many gifts back to Hungary as dowry for his little daughter. The ladies had brought their very finest garments so that they would look as good as the Hungarians. As soon as they saw the king's knights galloping to meet them on swift horses, they knew how right they had been. Such furs! Such velvet! So many jewels of enormous size! Such proudly waving eagle feathers! And these were only the knightly escorts for the guests. What would the royal court be like?

The visitors were soon to know. As the horses clattered over the drawbridge, trumpets sounded from every turret. Banners and pennants rippled in the light breeze, and servants sprang to assist the guests and lead them into the great hall. There, on their great throne, King Andrew and Queen Gertrude, with Elizabeth at their feet, sat waiting.

"How dark she is!" whispered one maiden to another.

"And how small!" said the other, trying not to look as if she were whispering.

The German maidens were tall and very fair, with long braids of golden hair. The little dark-haired princess with her olive skin was pretty, but decidedly not in the German way. Even though the child was half German, she did not look so, and the maidens shook their heads. They wondered what the landgrave would say.

Dame Bertha was determined to show these rich Hungarians that she, too, knew something about the way the ladies dressed in Paris. Packed in her chests and boxes were dresses of the finest silk, embroidered with gold thread. There was a red one almost covered with tiny thin gold circles, each one having a precious stone in the center. There was a cloak of royal blue with gold braid all around the edge—not just gilt but solid gold! It had circular clasps of gold set with sapphires, and the girdle was braided out of long strands of gold that reached to the very ground.

No one would be able to say that the ladies of Hungary outshone the ladies from Thuringia—not if Dame Bertha could help it.

She had her moments of doubt, however. Everything in this strange court seemed richer and more brilliant than anything she had known. The musicians played wild gypsy music that made the dances fast and exciting. The men lifted their partners high into the air, whirled them around, stamped, and shouted. The German girls could not keep up with them at all. They did not like that kind of dancing.

During the days of the German envoys' visit, every servant in the castle felt the rough edge of Queen Gertrude's tongue or a sharp cuff on the ear if anything went wrong.

There was some excuse for the queen. It was no easy task to rule over a household that included not only the large family and the knights who lived at the castle but hundreds of pages, squires, and servants of all ranks, as well as dozens of visitors, clergy, pilgrims, and traveling strangers. It was hard enough to provide food for such numbers, to say nothing of shelter and entertainment. Moreover, Queen Gertrude, who took part in many a political plot hatched by ambitious lords, had found nobles among the Thuringians who could be trusted to take certain messages back to Germany. She had other things on her mind besides housekeeping.

Right now there was one thing of special importance to attend to. Dozens of servants were busy preparing the splendid gifts that were to be sent back to Germany as dower for the little princess. Great metal boxes bound in brass were filled with bolts of rich silks and velvets for the ladies of the German court. Others held golden goblets set with jewels, beautifully made swords with jeweled scabbards, rings, bracelets, and necklaces. And that was not all. Some boxes contained yards of embroidered linen and rich hangings, while still others held quantities of fine furs.

When all the coaches were ready and the knights were trying to hold in check their spirited steeds, the little Princess Elizabeth was brought to the castle gate. She was dressed in rich, beautiful garments for the journey, and in the largest coach was placed a little silver cradle so that she might ride as comfortably as possible.

A number of Hungarian servants went along to take care of the little girl, and companies of knights were ready to ride at the beginning and the end of the cavalcade as escorts.

Elizabeth was usually a happy child, but all the excitement frightened her. She was too young to understand what lay before her, but she knew well enough that she was leaving her home and her parents and going to a strange place. With tears in her eyes she ran to her father to say good-bye.

"Act like a princess", said her mother sternly. "See that you do credit to your training when you reach the court of Thuringia."

King Andrew, however, took his little daughter in his arms and held her close. He looked around at the Thuringian knights, to whom he must now entrust the child, as if he were seeking a friendly face. At that moment Walter of Varila stepped forward—he of the kind, gray eyes and the gentle touch. Already he had felt drawn to the little girl and had decided to offer himself as her guardian. King Andrew looked at him and trusted him.

"Walter of Varila," he said solemnly, "to you I entrust my little daughter, and I beg you on your honor as a knight to defend her."

Walter of Varila reached out and took Elizabeth into his strong and steady arms.

"On my honor as a knight," he said, "I will protect Elizabeth, and as long as I live I will to this trust be faithful."

2

A NEW HOME AND A NEW FRIEND

"GOOD-BYE, little Elizabeth, good-bye. God go with you!"

"Oh, Stephen, must you go back? Can't you come all the way with me?"

"No, little lady. We must go back to the Pressburg. What would your father do without his knights?"

The Hungarian knights had come as far as the border with the German embassy, but now they had to return. It was time for Elizabeth to say farewell, and she very nearly forgot that she was a princess and that she must not cry.

Stephen lifted her in his arms, and she hugged him with all her might. Stephen was her favorite.

"There, now, little lady", he said, setting her down gently. "You have Guda with you. She will not let you be lonesome."

Guda was only a little older than Elizabeth and already lonesome herself, but she nodded solemnly and took Elizabeth's hand. Then Walter of Varila stepped forward and, with a cheerful, "In you go", swept Elizabeth and Guda into the coach beside Dame Bertha. The Hungarian knights raised their short swords in salute. Then they wheeled and galloped away, while Elizabeth waved from the window.

All along the way, when the people heard the coaches coming, they hurried out of their houses and shops and called a greeting to the princess. Church bells rang, trumpets blared from towers and balconies, and Elizabeth waved her hand and smiled as she had been taught to do.

"How dark her hair is!" whispered one housewife to another.

"It is easy to see that she is not one of ours", said another, shaking her head.

"Bless the poor little lamb! She has a sweet, happy

face", said the first speaker. "God give her good fortune."

"Welcome, welcome, in the name of God!" cried all
the people, and Elizabeth smiled her thanks.

By the time the embassy reached Eisenach, the little
village at the foot of the road to the Wartburg Castle, it
was twilight, and Elizabeth was very tired.

The cavalcade that rattled over the cobblestones
was much longer than the one that had gone for Elizabeth. Instead of two golden coaches, there were now
thirteen, most of them full of gifts. And there were a
number of fine Arabian horses for the landgrave's
family.

"Look out of the window, Elizabeth", said Dame
Bertha. "There is the Wartburg Castle. It is nearly dark
now, but you can easily see the tower above the trees."

Elizabeth looked up at the place she must now call
home. The castle stood high and proud on a mountain
top. In spite of the brightly colored banners flying in
welcome, it looked stark and grim. Around it the dark
Thuringian forest spread out over the whole countryside for more than a hundred miles.

As the coaches rolled over the drawbridge and up
the broad path to the castle, Elizabeth saw light stream-
ing from a wide door. Pages bearing torches ran to
meet them. In the doorway stood a large, bearded man
and a tall, fair boy with a gentle face.

"So this is Elizabeth! Welcome!" exclaimed Landgrave Hermann, reaching out his arms for the child.

He carried her into the great, dark hall and set her down in front of his wife, a handsome woman in rich attire. "She's not much bigger than a squirrel."

Landgravine Sophie smiled at Elizabeth and turned to the fair-haired boy. "This is Louis, Elizabeth—and here are Agnes and Hermann, who will play with you, too. You will see the younger boys tomorrow."

Louis stepped forward and looked down at the bewildered child. He took her by the hand.

"You are very tired, aren't you?" he said. "My mother will give you some supper, and then she will put you to bed. Tomorrow I will show you the castle."

Elizabeth did not understand all the words, although she had learned some German from her mother, but she knew that Louis was good and kind. She smiled at him and felt happy.

From the very beginning Louis was Elizabeth's refuge. He became her firmest friend and champion. Although he was six years older than Elizabeth, he loved the little princess from the first time he saw her. There was something very appealing in her shy smile and in her dark hair and eyes.

Louis was tall and fair. So were his sister, Agnes, and his brothers. Elizabeth was different, and he liked her. "Little Sister" he called her, and she called him "Brother". He took her by the hand and suited his longer steps to her short ones. Whenever she was hurt or frightened, she ran to Louis.

"Don't cry, little Sister", he would say.

Elizabeth would dry her tears and smile at him.

"I won't cry, dear Brother."

Elizabeth was often frightened. The castle was dark and noisy. The walls were very thick, and the staircases were long, dark, and steep.

Knights, squires, and pages scurried about, some preparing to ride to a tournament at a neighboring castle, some getting ready to go hawking or hunting wild boar in the forest, still others arranging one of the great halls for dancing or the coming of minstrels.

The baying of hounds echoed through the passages as pages held the dogs in leash. Everyone was shouting orders to someone else, and the horses pranced and curveted in excitement.

"How beautiful the horses are!" thought the little princess. She had the Hungarian love of fine horses. Every day, back at home, some knight would reach down as he galloped by and lift her to his saddle. Then they would ride and ride, far into the distance, with the golden wheat fields shining beside them and the wind blowing Elizabeth's hair and the long white plume of the knight who held her. Here in this dark castle, wherever she went she ran into a wall. Elizabeth felt shut in.

The little girl's education began at once. Landgravine Sophie was a good woman, and, in her way, she was kind to the little stranger. It was her duty, however, to train the child properly so that she would be a good ruler when she grew up. The landgravine was very busy, too, keeping track of all the servants and running her huge household.

In the Middle Ages women of the nobility did not have an easy life. They had to know how to manage the great estates when their husbands were away on crusades or on military duty. They were taught to do fine embroidery, to sing and to play upon some musical instrument, and to ride horseback. Nearly all of these skills the landgravine herself would have to teach to little Elizabeth.

"Have you finished your embroidery, Elizabeth?"

"Go now, Elizabeth, and practice on your lute."

"Stand straight, Elizabeth. A princess must never look tired."

So many things to learn. So many things to teach. And the landgravine had other things to worry about. Landgrave Hermann was in constant trouble. He was restless and undecided. Sometimes he rode away with a company of knights and was gone for weeks, burning villages, plundering castles, and adding new vassals to his large estates.

Sometimes it was the other way around, and the Wartburg was attacked with arrows and battering rams. Fires lighted up the dark forest, and everyone in the castle had to hide except the fighting men.

Such an attack occurred one day when Louis and Elizabeth were down in the courtyard watching the knights practice for a coming tournament. Suddenly there was a terrible commotion. Everything seemed to happen at once. The whole world was full of galloping horsemen and flying arrows tipped with flame. The alarm bell sounded, and the portcullis dropped with a frightening clang.

"Oh, Louis, what is it?" Elizabeth clutched the boy's arm in terror.

In another second Walter of Varila was at her side. He snatched her up into his saddle and galloped toward the castle entrance. There he set her down and thrust her inside the door. "Go straight to the women's room", he directed her sternly and was gone.

Another knight, riding at full speed, had lifted Louis to his saddle. Now he dropped his young master unceremoniously at the door and galloped off to the defense of the castle.

"Where are you, little Sister?" called Louis anxiously, but Elizabeth was right beside him. The two children started up the steep, dark stairs, but when they came to one of the narrow, deep windows, Louis looked out to see how the battle was going.

"Let me see, too, Brother", pleaded Elizabeth as he held her back. Elizabeth must always do what Louis did. She pushed her head up under his arm and stared out in fear and horror.

The woods below were aflame. Bodies of fallen knights lay in the courtyard in pools of blood. Enemy soldiers were trying to scale the walls with ladders while the Wartburg defenders hurled flaming weapons at them and held them back with swords and arrows.

Louis wanted to watch because he wanted to know how to defend the castle when he became landgrave, but first he must take Elizabeth to his mother

"Stay here, little Sister, and you will be safe", he said when they reached the women's room. He would have gone back to watch the battle, but his mother made him stay with her. Louis was not yet old enough for war.

This particular battle did not last very long, and the Wartburg knights easily routed the enemy, but it was Elizabeth's first, and she never forgot it.

When those warlike times were over, Hermann wanted the whole castle to be joyful. He loved beautiful things. Everything used in the castle was rich and handsome. Poets and musicians were always welcome, because Hermann wanted a lively and brilliant court.

Landgravine Sophie arranged everything as he wanted it, but in her heart was fear. She knew that at any time her husband might be excommunicated because of his quarrels with Church authorities. Elizabeth did not understand all the landgravine's worries, but she was quick to sense trouble. She tried to make things easier for the landgravine by being strictly obedient herself.

When Elizabeth first came to Thuringia, Landgrave Hermann decided that she would need girls of her own age to play with. His own daughter, Agnes, who was nearly the same age, would, of course, be first choice. Then there was Guda, faithful Guda who had come with Elizabeth from Hungary. She was a year older. Little yellow-haired Isentrude, daughter of a Thuringian noble, was about a year younger. Altogether there were seven who played together constantly.

One of their favorite games was played with a large, soft, red ball. The girls would stand in a wide circle with one girl in the middle. One of the others would throw the ball to the middle girl. If she caught it, she tossed it back to someone else in the ring. If she missed, she had to run and hide while the girls counted to ten. If she were caught, she had to pay a forfeit.

One day when the girls were playing, Elizabeth invited a little village girl who was passing to play with them.

"Why do you always want to play with beggars and servants?" asked Agnes angrily. "You do not act like a princess at all."

"But they like to play, too", protested Elizabeth. "They would be just like us if they weren't poor."

"Well, I won't play if she does", announced Agnes, and most of the girls followed her lead. Only Guda and Isentrude stayed with Elizabeth, although they were afraid of Agnes.

Elizabeth fought back the tears. She turned to the little visitor. "I am sorry that we can't have a game, but here is a little present for you." She took a jeweled bracelet from her wrist and gave it to the child, who took it and ran away with a frightened thank you.

"I'm going to tell Mother," said Agnes as she started toward the castle, "and I'll tell on you, too, Isentrude." Agnes was always happy to "tell on" Elizabeth or those who sided with her.

Elizabeth learned German quickly, but when she felt lonesome for her old home she and Guda talked together in Hungarian. Guda was often lonesome, too.

"I miss the sunny wheat fields", Guda would say. "And I miss my mother at night."

"The forest is dark and frightening," Elizabeth agreed, "and I would like to hear the gypsies play the *czardas* again."

In spite of her loneliness and Agnes' spiteful tongue, Elizabeth remained an unusually merry and generous child. She loved to share her lovely toys with the other girls. She liked to race up and down the long corridors, her dark curls bobbing and her dark eyes laughing. She was always ready for fun.

Louis took her all over the castle. He was very serious about it. Someday she would be the Lady of the Wartburg, and she would have to know every inch of the castle when she ruled over it. Up and down the steep stairs Elizabeth trudged wherever Louis led her.

"See, this is the Knights' Hall. This is where I practice with my lance and sword."

Elizabeth peered into the big room, noisy with the clank of metal. All around the hall hung suits of armor. Swords, lances, and pennons hung in their proper places. Some of the knights were resting. Some were playing chess. Others were polishing armor or practicing with the broadsword.

"Are you a knight, Louis?"

"No, little Sister, I am only a page, but soon I shall be a squire. Then I can serve my father. I shall carve his meat at the table and stand behind him at the councils. I shall take care of his horse and ride behind him in battle."

Elizabeth's eyes clouded.

"Must you go to war soon, Louis?"

"Oh, no, not for a long time. I have not learned enough yet, but when I do go, I will bring you back a present."

"Oh, will you, Brother? What will the present be?"

"It will be a surprise. You mustn't ask."

"Then I will not ask—but I will guess."

Elizabeth's eyes danced again. Anything Louis wanted, Elizabeth wanted.

At first the ladies of the castle made a pet of Elizabeth. She was so little and so cheerful although she was so far away from home. Then they began to be annoyed at her. She was always praying, or performing little penances, or giving away the things she cherished most. She loved God so much that the others were almost frightened. Besides, she made them uncomfortable. Maybe they weren't doing as much as they should for God. Some of them spoke very unkindly about Elizabeth, and the landgravine often reproved her sharply.

"She has given away all her own jewels. Now she is beginning on things that do not belong to her."

"The landgravine will attend to that. I have heard her say that Elizabeth must be punished if she continues. Why, she even goes to the kitchen and fills great baskets so full of food that she can hardly carry them and takes them down to the gate to the beggars."

"Hoping that someone will see her, I suppose, and think how holy she is!"

"Well, she may find herself in trouble. Her mother never did send the money and the gold and silver plate that she promised when Elizabeth came here."

"Didn't Elizabeth have any dowry?"

"Oh, yes. It was quite generous, I believe, but Queen Gertrude said that she would double it in a year or two, and she has not kept her promise. She probably never intended to do so. Elizabeth is really not a good match for our Louis."

So went the court gossip, and even though the little girl did not understand all of it, her heart was often heavy.

"They don't like me here, Guda", she said to her Hungarian companion.

"But, Elizabeth, you do spend a great deal of time praying in the chapel. Do you think you should go there so often?"

Faithful Guda was worried by the constant criticism of the court ladies. Even Walter of Varila, who always defended Elizabeth, could not silence some of the sharp tongues. The seven little girls continued to play together, but, as they grew older, they noticed something different about Elizabeth.

She often knelt in the chapel for an hour or more with eyes fixed intently on the crucifix over the altar. Her lips moved as if she were conversing with Christ himself. Only Guda knew how real these visions were to Elizabeth and how frequently they occurred, but she never told anyone until long, long after.

Even when she was quite a little girl, Elizabeth thought of the chapel as home. She went in whenever she could and told God about all the things that happened to her. She sang to him the Latin hymns that she had learned. When she was quite sure that she was alone, she even brought her lute to his feet and played him a little tune. Even before she could read, she would take the big missal that the priests used and lay it on the top step of the altar. It was a very beautiful book with thick pages, covered with big black music notes and ornamented with rich and shining color.

"Here is your beautiful book, dear God", Elizabeth would say, opening it to a lovely page. "I would like to read it to you, but I do not understand the words, so please read it to yourself, dear God."

Of all the things in the chapel, however, it was the crucifix that most attracted Elizabeth's attention. When she looked at the crucifix, she felt helpless to tell her Savior how much she loved him. He died for the sins of the world. What could a little girl do to show her thanks?

She tried to suffer patiently small hurts or injuries without mentioning them. She gave up her turn in the games to Agnes or Isentrude. She stopped playing a game just when she was winning. She ate things that she did not like and gave away the little prizes she received for learning her lessons well. All she ever asked in return was a Hail Mary, and she always told those who received her gifts not to thank her, but God.

When the children played ball or tag in the long halls, Elizabeth invented ways of getting close to the chapel so that she could get in, or look in, or at least touch the door. Then she could feel as if God were touching her. Everything she did was for God. Every hour was long if she had no time to talk to God.

And because Elizabeth was generous with him, God was already bestowing on her, in secret, rich gifts of which not even she was aware. God had begun already to make her a saint, and it was not long before he asked of her greater sacrifices than any she had yet made for his sake.

One day there came dreadful news to the castle. A messenger from Hungary galloped up to the heavy gate where triple guards were always stationed. He had ridden night and day and could hardly hold himself erect in his saddle. The guards lowered their lances as he showed his papers, and the drawbridge dropped with a clang to admit him. One squire took the traveler's weary horse, and another led him to the landgrave.

Queen Gertrude, Elizabeth's mother, was dead. She had been murdered, probably by someone at the Hungarian court who had been angered by her political schemes. She had never been popular in Hungary, partly because she was German and partly because the people did not trust her. They were disappointed in King Andrew, too, and ashamed of him because he had not kept his promise to lead a crusade to the Holy Land.

"Poor little one!" said someone. "It is hard enough for a child when a mother dies—but murder! How will she take it?"

"She had little enough affection from her mother", said Dame Bertha of Bendeleiben. She remembered Queen Gertrude's stern command to her little daughter as they left the Pressburg Castle. "She will soon forget."

"And who, now, will keep the queen's promise to send more gold and silver for Elizabeth's dowry?"

"Not King Andrew! He is already in debt up to his ears."

"Still, we should pity the queen", added one more friendly voice. "She was murdered. She died without the Sacrament. We should pray for her soul."

The whole court of Landgrave Hermann did indeed go into mourning, as was proper for the mother of the future landgravine. The great bell tolled solemnly, and everyone in the castle knelt to pray for the soul of Queen Gertrude.

Elizabeth was too young to understand all that the older people were saying, but she knew that her mother was dead. She must pray constantly for her mother's soul.

"Do you remember my mother, Guda?"

"Yes, Elizabeth."

"Will you always, always pray for her soul? Promise?"

"I promise, Elizabeth, I will not forget."

In spite of the fact that, for a while, the ladies of the court were kinder to her because of her mother's death, Elizabeth knew well that they did not approve of her. They showed it in many ways. They had always criticized her for being too charitable and too religious, but she was getting old enough now to understand that they did not even consider her a suitable wife for Louis.

Guda did not want to tell Elizabeth that a great many people were advising the landgravine to send her back to her father and to choose a German girl for Louis. Agnes, however, did not mind hurting Elizabeth's feelings.

"They'll send you back to Hungary. You'll see. I know all about it", said Agnes, who liked to pretend that she knew everything that went on in the castle.

During all these early years of unhappiness and misunderstanding, Elizabeth continued to take all her troubles to God. Sometimes she ran to her good friend Walter of Varila and cried herself out in his arms. But Louis could always make the sun come out. Louis never failed her. When she saw him coming, she ran as fast as she could and threw her arms around his neck.

"Why were you so long in coming, Brother?"

"You are so impatient, little Sister."

"Have you a present for me, Louis?"

"Yes, hold out your hand."

It might be only a flower, or a shining stone, or a small bit of jewelry, but if Louis gave it to her it was a treasure. She would never go back to Hungary and leave Louis, Elizabeth thought to herself. Never! Never! She belonged to Louis, and he belonged to her. That was what God wanted. Elizabeth was sure.

And God was training Louis, too, to be a strong support for Elizabeth in later days of trouble. Louis loved Elizabeth and understood her. She was cheerful and happy whenever Louis was near. But already dark clouds of misfortune were gathering over the Wartburg Castle, and both Louis and Elizabeth would have great need of comfort.

3

DARKER TIMES

WHILE ELIZABETH AND LOUIS were growing up in the Wartburg Castle, they often heard stories about the young emperor, Frederick II, who was a cousin of Landgrave Hermann. Every boy of Louis' age wanted to be a knight like Frederick. He was handsome, clever, courageous, and very much admired wherever he went. Even as a small child his life had been exciting and colorful.

Perhaps the children's favorite story about Frederick was the one describing a terrible night in his childhood. A band of fierce Saracens, armed with wicked curved scimitars, attacked the old Norman castle at Palermo in Sicily where five-year-old Frederick was staying. German and Sicilian Christians were defending the castle, but they were driven out by the Saracens. Somehow, in the confusion, the little boy was left alone in the dark, with the enemy pouring in at the gate.

One of the minstrels would often repeat the story at the children's request as he entertained the family and guests after the evening meal. While the gold flame of the torches lighted up the shadowy corners, Louis and Elizabeth would lean forward with rapt attention as the minstrel raised his voice dramatically:

"The frightened child ran back and forth through the halls, screaming and crying for help. At last, hungry and cold and desperate, he hid in the darkest corner of the great living hall. Suddenly, a torch flamed in the darkness, and a number of Saracens entered. Although Frederick expected to be killed, he was proud and valiant even then. He dried his tears and stood up straight, but the Saracens did not touch him. Out of their wide sleeves they brought food and drink, and they placed it before him with a low bow. Then they disappeared into the darkness.

"Just think how brave he was!" Louis would say. "If I could only be like Frederick!"

"You are brave!" Elizabeth assured him loyally. "You will be the bravest knight in the whole world."

Emperor Frederick was tall and red-haired like his grandfather. He had been brought up among warriors and had become self-willed and defiant, but he could be very gracious and charming too. At thirteen, he was king of Sicily. At fifteen, he was married. At seventeen, he was emperor of the Holy Roman Empire. That was a great responsibility for a boy of seventeen, but in many ways he was like his famous grandfather, Frederick Barbarossa. Already he was a person of power and influence. Like all the other young nobles, Louis hoped some day to serve under him, perhaps even to follow him in a crusade. Little did Louis or Elizabeth know then of the part Frederick would have in their lives.

The children who lived in the Wartburg Castle heard a great deal about the crusades from travelers, minstrels, and from actual crusaders. Many stopped at the castle for shelter on their journeys. There were the Hospitallers of the Order of St. John, who had been organized after the First Crusade to take care of the poor and sick. They usually wore black cloaks with a white cross, but the ones who fought against the Turks wore red surcoats with a white cross over their armor and a big red mantle with a white cross.

"How I should like to be a Hospitaller!" said Elizabeth. "Then I could take care of the wounded knights."

"But you are a girl, little Sister. You cannot go to the Holy Land."

"Then I will stay at home and build a hospital to take care of all the wounded crusaders", said Elizabeth.

"I want to be a Knight Templar", declared Louis. The Templars were his great heroes. They were a band of very rich nobles who built a house close to the Temple in Jerusalem and fought to save the Holy Sepulcher. They called themselves Templars or Knights of the Temple and wore white surcoats and mantles with great red crosses.

"Tell me how the knights take the cross, Louis."

"I have told you a dozen times, little Sister."

"Tell me again. I like to hear it."

So Louis told her again how a big tournament was held at some castle and how the bishop came with the holy relics.

"Then the trumpets sound," said Louis, "and the heralds call upon all the knights to take the cross if they want to serve God and save their souls. Then the leaders go up and kiss the crucifix, and the bishop blesses them and fastens red crosses on their shoulders."

"Do all the knights take the cross, Brother?"

"Most of them do. Of course, the bishops want only the bravest knights who love God very much. It is a very hard journey to the Holy Land."

"You will go someday, won't you, Brother?"

"Of course I will. I think about it very often. I want to see Jerusalem and the Mount of Olives and the Sea of Galilee. I know it will be hard. You have heard yourself that many crusaders die of plagues and fevers before they even get to Jerusalem. Some have been lost at sea, too. I think it is better to die fighting the Turks and Saracens hand to hand with a broadsword, but it is not important. The bishops say that he who loses his life for the love of God will save it for all eternity. It does not matter how we die if it is for the love of God."

The love of God. That was something Elizabeth could understand.

"Do you remember the stranger who told us about the Children's Crusade, Brother?"

"I remember well. How I wanted to be like Nicholas of Cologne and lead a crusade to the Holy Land— and he was only ten years old! I was just about the same age then."

Neither Elizabeth nor Louis could forget the thrilling story about the children who started a crusade because their elders were too busy fighting with each other to heed the Pope's call for leaders. Nicholas of Cologne gathered hundreds of children in the Rhineland and drilled them like a company of knights. He said that an angel had ordered him to free the holy places. Finally, there were thousands of children marching across the Alps to Genoa, singing hymns and praising God. Nobody could stop them. One little French shepherd boy brought a banner with a lamb embroidered on it. The banner said: "O Lord Christ, restore to us thy Cross."

It was a long time afterward that the people at the Wartburg heard what became of the children. Many died of cold and hunger, and others were sold as slaves to the Saracens. Very few returned to their homes. They died for the love of God. How much Elizabeth wanted to do something great for the love of God! She thought a great deal about those brave and holy children and wished that she could have gone with them.

Elizabeth loved Louis more than anyone else in the world. Louis never laughed at her or made fun of her, because she liked to do little things for God. He knew what she was doing when she made excuses to get closer to the chapel. She would run in, pretending she had dropped her ball, and say a quick prayer or kiss the wall of God's house. Louis didn't mind if she gave away the little presents he brought her. He even helped her carry baskets of food to the beggars at the gate.

Every year, on the night before Advent, the children of the castle drew lots to decide upon special patron saints for the year. Each child chose two or three saints' names to be used for the ceremony, so it sometimes happened that the same name was repeated several times. One year Louis, as the oldest, held a silver bowl full of small candles, on each of which a saint's name was written, and each child took three turns. Elizabeth drew the name of Saint John three times in succession.

"Saint John must be your true patron saint", said Isentrude.

"But Elizabeth is already dedicated to our Lady", objected Guda.

"Oh, our Lady won't mind", said Elizabeth. "She loved Saint John because he was close to our Savior. He will keep me close to God, too."

As Louis grew older, he didn't have time to be with Elizabeth so much. He was being trained as the future ruler of Thuringia, and he had a great many things to learn. The pages in the Wartburg Castle were very strictly trained from the age of seven. They were taught modesty, truth, and good manners according to rigid rules. A page had to know how to serve the lords and ladies properly in any situation. He had to keep himself clean and neat, and he was never allowed to laugh or joke noisily.

Louis learned to play chess and backgammon, to sing a little, and to play on a small harp. He studied Latin and French and learned enough mathematics to keep the complex accounts of a great feudal castle. He learned to swim, to draw a straight bow, to fight expertly with sword or lance, to hurl javelins, and, of course, to ride so well that no other knight could unseat him or surpass him in the lists.

Of all the boys in the castle, Louis was the most promising. He was greatly gifted both physically and mentally, and he learned from Elizabeth to perform every action for the love of God. No one else knew about it. It was their secret.

"Everything for God, Brother!"

"Everything for God, little Sister!"

Elizabeth worked industriously at her sewing and embroidery because she wanted to make beautiful tunics and cloaks and surcoats for Louis. There were many tailors working in the castle, but Louis loved best the garments that Elizabeth made for him so lovingly. Like all the pages, he wore long tightfitting hose. His sleeveless tunic or jacket had long sleeves hanging in points to his knees. On his blond, bobbed hair he wore a little embroidered cap or a wide, soft velvet hat. Elizabeth liked to make the caps and to fashion long bands of matching embroidery for his sleeves. Already she was thinking ahead to the fine clothes he would need as a squire and later, when he became a knight. Her knight! Next to God came Louis, and already God was training the boy's mind and soul so that he would be worthy of her.

Louis was fortunate. He was the very image of the medieval knight. Everyone in the castle loved him and approved of him. As soon as he was seventeen, he would become a true knight, and the people would be able to present him proudly to Thuringia and to the world as their prince and their ruler. With Elizabeth it was different. She had come as a stranger to the castle, and in many ways she had remained a stranger.

In spite of the unkindness of Agnes, who had never liked her, and the jealousy of others, Elizabeth did enjoy life. She had a good deal of her mother in her, and she put her whole being into everything she did. She loved jokes, and she hated the artificial manners of the court ladies. They painted their faces and spent hours twining ribbons, or long strands of gold, into the braids of hair that hung over their shoulders and down to their knees. They bought beauty lotions from the peddlers who came to the castle. Most of their time was spent in practicing new dance steps and talking about their favorite knights. The preachers often gave sermons about too much concern with fashion. They scolded the ladies for spending so much time trying to make themselves look different from the way God made them.

Elizabeth liked to play hard, but it was not easy to play in the clothes children wore in those days. She wore a long, tight slip of white linen with narrow, uncomfortable sleeves. Her long straight dress was of heavy wool or velvet, with a wide belt or girdle that fastened with a big gold buckle. The outer sleeves were very wide and had points hanging almost to the ground.

When she went outdoors, Elizabeth had a wide, heavy cloak that covered her completely. Cloaks worn indoors were not so heavy, and all the ladies spent a great deal of time practicing how to manage them gracefully. Elizabeth thought all of this attention to unimportant matters very silly, and she was often scolded for not getting things right.

"The ends of your girdle are not tied properly, Elizabeth."

"When you make a curtsy, hold your skirt wide this way. Some day you may meet the emperor. Then you will be glad that you know how to behave."

Elizabeth really loved pretty clothes because Louis loved them. She wanted very much to do everything properly, even the things she hated most, so that she would be a credit to Louis. As she grew older, this thought became increasingly important to her. She would look into the mirror and wonder if Louis would think her pretty. Then right afterward she would accuse herself of vanity and punish herself severely in some way that nobody would notice. Louis did not think very much about it. From the beginning there had never been anyone but Elizabeth for him. He liked her just the way she was.

Landgravine Sophie tried to be fair in spite of the court gossip. Elizabeth had never fitted into the life of the court as had been expected. King Andrew had never made good the promises of Queen Gertrude to send more money for Elizabeth's dowry. More than one person had advised Sophie to send the girl home, but Louis was getting old enough now to defend her. He had no intention of letting Elizabeth be sent away. Sophie could get no help from her husband, either. The landgrave was in trouble. His knights no longer rode off to battle. The emperor had not rewarded the landgrave for his help, and Hermann began to make alliances with other leaders. He sat brooding darkly in his great chair, and the castle was silent.

Then suddenly the blow fell. Landgrave Hermann was excommunicated. Elizabeth was nine and Louis fifteen when it happened. The whole castle was terror-stricken. The landgrave was crazed with fear. He beat his head on the stone floor. The landgravine could not help him. No one could help him.

Now the chapel was closed. The Host was taken from the tabernacle by a priest sent by the bishop. Elizabeth knelt on the floor and watched, too stunned for tears. The door of the tabernacle was left open. Stark emptiness. God had left his home in the chapel. What would they do without him? The altar cloths were folded away. The candles burned no more. The chapel was just another room.

Elizabeth tried to comfort Louis, but she needed comforting herself. No one would come to visit them lest the curse strike others, too. The face of God was hidden from all in the Wartburg Castle, and Elizabeth was crushed. Her whole world was shattered.

The landgrave sat stricken and speechless in his council room. Louis stood beside him and spoke for him. Louis signed the papers and documents. He became his father's voice and pen. He and Elizabeth clung to each other in their sorrow.

"Do not leave me, little Sister."

"I will never leave you, Brother."

At night the landgrave had bad dreams and roared aloud in fear and anguish. Sophie never left his side. One night he dreamed that the Blessed Virgin and

Saint Catherine told him to build a convent in Eisenach. He was much comforted. Perhaps he might save his soul after all. He and Sophie made immediate plans and built a convent in Eisenach in honor of Saint Catherine. The abbess and the nuns who were placed in charge promised to pray for his soul, and the landgrave ordered that all of his family should be buried there.

Not long afterward, misfortune struck again. Young Hermann died—Hermann, the brother of Louis and nearest to him in age—Hermann who had been Elizabeth's playmate. There he lay, white as wax against the black of the funeral bier. No use to take him to the chapel. God was not there. The children covered him with flowers, and a company of knights carried him down the steep path to Eisenach.

The death of Hermann was the first that had touched Elizabeth closely. The beauty of the Requiem Mass filled her soul with warm comfort. God was in this chapel at Saint Catherine's. He had already sent his angels down to take Hermann up to heaven. The boy's body would lie forever under Saint Catherine's altar, but his soul would be with God. Elizabeth wished that her own soul could go to God right then. But God was not ready.

Now the landgrave's mind was weighted down by grief and fear. At night he thought he was pursued by demons, and the whole castle shuddered to hear his piercing screams. The man was sick in mind and body.

He seldom tried to lift his weary body to the saddle now, but one day, when he did ride forth, death rode with him, and his sorrowing knights bore him home for the last time.

Everyone remembered now what he had been like when the Wartburg was a happy castle, when God lived in the lovely chapel and minstrels sang in the great halls. There were many monks and nuns who prayed for the landgrave's soul and chanted the Holy Office.

Long years afterward, Elizabeth's friend Isentrude told how Elizabeth and Louis often prayed for the landgrave's soul and how they wept over the prayer that Louis found one day written in his mother's psalter:

"To thee, Jesus, I commend the soul of thy servant, Hermann, who, although he is entangled in crime and sin, is still thy creature for whom the sacred blood of Christ was shed and who sets his hopes upon thee. Deliver him from evil today and always. Render him free from the power, the missiles, and the force of his foes. Save him from shame of the body and from sudden death. I commend him to thee in the hope and faith that he may be saved. Hear me, a poor sinner, plead for thy brother Hermann."

4

A CROWN OF GOLD
FOR A CROWN OF THORNS

TA-RA-TA! TA-RA-TA! Ta-ra, ta-ra, ta-ra!
The joyful sound of a horn proclaimed the return
of Prince Louis. Across the courtyard raced a bright
little figure, skirts lifted, curls flying. That was Elizabeth. As soon as the prince dismounted, she threw herself into his arms, and he held her tight, careful not to
hurt her with his heavy gauntlets.

"Oh, Brother, I am so glad to see you. Where is my present?"

"I haven't any present for you this time."

"Oh, Louis!"

Louis couldn't bear to see the light fade from Elizabeth's eyes.

"Smile again, little Sister. You know I would not forget you—but you cannot have your present now. It is in my saddle-bags, and my horse has already gone to the stable. I have a roll of beautiful silk for you—enough for a gown and a cloak."

"Oh, Louis, how lovely! What color?"

"Gold, little Sister. Nothing else is good enough for you."

Elizabeth's eyes were dancing again.

"And are we going to the fair, Louis?"

"The fair? What fair?"

"Oh, Brother! You *know* that the fair begins tomorrow in Eisenach. You signed the permission papers yourself. Don't you remember? It's the fair for the Cistercian Abbey."

"Tomorrow? Yes, I had forgotten. Very well, little Sister. Tell everyone to be ready at seven. I'll give orders to have the coaches prepared. I suppose you want to go to Mass at Saint Catherine's?"

"Oh, yes, Louis."

As a matter of fact, it was Mass at Saint Catherine's that Elizabeth wanted more than to visit the fair. She loved to go to Mass in Eisenach, and, besides Mass at

Saint Catherine's, she would almost certainly get a chance to visit the chapel at the Cistercian Abbey and possibly even one of the other churches. It would be like a little pilgrimage. That meant happiness for Elizabeth.

All the people in the castle liked to go to a fair. They could be sure of color and excitement. Even Landgravine Sophie, still in heavy mourning, forgot her troubles for a little while as she watched the jugglers and mimes or listened to the gleemen.

Louis was landgrave of Thuringia now. He was still only a boy, but he had been well trained. Already he had made a reputation for honesty and truth, and he was highly regarded by other rulers in spite of his youth. He had often heard the stories of King Arthur told by the minstrels, and he always kept in his heart the ideal of a perfect knight. Like his father, however, he was a shrewd politician, and he managed the affairs of his kingdom as well as did the older rulers with whom he had to deal.

Promptly at seven the next morning the coaches were at the gates. After Mass everyone went out into the village to look at the fair. All around the village green were little booths full of things to be sold. Some of the booths were built of light wood, some of canvas, and some were just little shelters of branches. The pitchmen were shouting to attract attention to their wares.

"Finest singing birds! Beautiful singing birds."

"Peacock pie! Peacock pie! Don't leave the fair until you have tasted my peacock pie!"

Men were driving herds of cattle and horses to the animal market. There was a bird market where geese and swans, pheasants and peacocks were sold. There were two or three cages of wild animals too, at which the village children gazed in fear and awe.

"Oh, the monkeys! See the dear little monkeys!"

Elizabeth loved the grave-faced little monkey in the red cap and coat that jumped into her arms and held out his cap for a coin. She hugged him and gave him a whole handful of coins because he looked so sad.

Mud. Mud. Mud. Everywhere there was mud. Wooden planks were laid down over the worst places, but there was little room to pass. The ladies from the castle held up their skirts and found it difficult to keep their balance and keep their clothes out of the puddles. As Elizabeth crossed one bad place, a man jostled her rudely and pushed her into the mud. Louis was angry and wanted to punish the man at once, but Elizabeth stopped him.

"No, Brother. He had just as much right to walk on the plank as I did", she said. "God wants us to suffer such little humiliations for his sake. Think how he was treated in the court of Pilate."

The merchants were glad to see the landgravine and her household because she often made large purchases. Sometimes her stewards bought a whole year's supply of spiced wine or enough linen to supply the castle for months. They bought oil and honey, salt fish, and tallow for daily needs. And the ladies, of course, bought cloaks, veils, silks, embroideries, and jewelry. The knights were interested in armor and leather goods, in saddles and trappings for their horses.

After the nobles had made their purchases, they went to the village green to see what entertainment could be found. Elizabeth's eyes sparkled at the unfamiliar sights. There were dwarfs and giants pretending to wrestle with each other, trained dogs and bears, ballad-singers, and jugglers. One of them especially delighted her.

"Watch him, Brother, watch him!" she cried, wanting Louis to share her pleasure.

The juggler kept ten golden balls in the air and never dropped one. Then he balanced a long gilded stick on his chin and slowly, slowly, without once disturbing the stick, first knelt, then sat, and finally lay down flat on the ground. Then he rose again in the same cautious fashion until he was standing perfectly straight, except for his head, which was still bent back balancing the stick. He lifted the stick from his chin and bowed to the ladies of the court with a great flourish, spreading his scarlet cloak out wide. Elizabeth had been holding her own breath. She never thought that the juggler could keep that stick on his chin until he was back on his feet again. She tossed him a golden coin in appreciation. Then she closed her eyes and said a little prayer of thanksgiving to God for all the pleasures he gave her.

When the time came to go home, Elizabeth insisted that the girls go with her to the cemetery. Guda and Isentrude were willing, but the others were beginning to think Elizabeth really tiresome.

"You have already been to Mass, and you went to the Cistercian Abbey after that. Now it's the cemetery! We are all tired, and it's time to go home", said one of the girls.

"If you're going to act like a nun all the time, why don't you go and ask the nuns to take you in?" asked another crossly.

But Elizabeth had her way. Agnes could hardly refuse, because Elizabeth prayed more for the landgrave's soul than she, his own daughter, did.

"We must never forget to pray for the holy souls", said Elizabeth earnestly when they reached the cemetery. "They need our help now, but some day we shall need *their* prayers."

In the thirteenth century, children did not receive Holy Communion until the age of twelve, but so great was Elizabeth's longing to be close to God that he showed himself to her on several occasions. Guda knew, but nobody else, that Elizabeth had actually seen a vision of Christ one day. She was feeding the poor at the gate of the castle when suddenly he stood among them. As she fell to her knees in astonishment and awe, he placed his hands upon those who stood near him, and all at once they, too, had the face of Christ. He was telling her that she must see his face in every one of the poor, the ugly, the sick, and the deformed.

Up to that time Elizabeth had tried not to look at the sores of the beggars. She had been taught to care for the sick and wounded, but, in spite of her compassion, she had been always repelled by dirt and ugliness and the sight of open sores. Now she knew that as soon as she possibly could she must go out and nurse the sick and afflicted. She must see Christ's face in that of each of his suffering children.

About this time something happened that greatly disturbed the landgravine and, in fact, the whole castle. It was the custom for the entire court to attend Mass at Saint Catherine's in Eisenach on Sundays and feast days.

The landgravine, in spite of her mourning, was conscious of the fact that she made a striking picture as she entered the church with the two beautiful young princesses beside her. She always insisted that they wear their newest and finest garments, although Elizabeth protested. She thought that it was not proper to distract the attention of the congregation from God on his altar throne.

It was the feast of the Assumption, and the landgravine, with the two princesses clad in their beautiful garments, entered the church and moved up the broad aisle to the high altar. The landgravine had laid aside her mourning for the feast day and wore the golden crown that proclaimed her queen of Thuringia. Agnes and Elizabeth wore small golden coronets set with jewels.

All three knelt and crossed themselves. The landgravine and Agnes bowed their heads in prayer, but Elizabeth looked up at the crucifix, and her Savior looked down at her. Suddenly she had another vision. She thought that the Blood of Jesus flowed down from his wounded hand and his heart and gathered in a little pool at her feet. She looked at the crown of thorns that her Savior wore, and she thought of her own rich garments and her golden crown. How could she wear a crown of gold while Jesus Christ, who died for her, was wearing a cruel crown of thorns? Her eyes filled with tears. Her heart seemed almost as if it would burst with love for her Savior. She snatched the crown from her head and laid it on the altar step. Then she bowed down to the floor in adoration while her body shook with sobs.

The landgravine turned and saw Elizabeth half kneeling, half lying on the step, her veil loosened and her crown before her. She was furious at the sight, but she tried to keep the knights and ladies who had followed them from noticing. She pulled Elizabeth up straight and helped her to replace the crown, as if it had fallen by accident. But she could not hide the tears of the princess, and she could not take from the girl's heart the image of her crucified Savior, who was calling her more and more frequently. Just what God wanted of her she wasn't sure, but, whatever it was, she was ready to give it to him with all her heart.

The little scene at the altar had not passed unno-
ticed, however, as the landgravine had hoped. It caused
a great deal of talk in the castle. It was bad enough that
Elizabeth should invite the children from the village to
come up to the castle to play with her. She behaved
like a serving wench, the ladies said. She was not a true
princess. She must be the child of some poor peasants,
pretending to be a princess. But even if she were the
daughter of King Andrew, what about him? He was no
father to be proud of.

A pilgrim stopping at the castle for rest and refresh-
ment had brought bad news of King Andrew. He had
finally been forced to keep his promise to go on a crusade to the Holy Land. He was actually the leader of a
large group for a while, but he was half-hearted about
the whole thing. He went only because of his promise
to his dying father. He did not want to attack. Instead
of leading his knights to battle against the Saracens, he
made a peaceful expedition across the plains of Jericho
and up to the shores of the Red Sea. As a leader, Andrew was weak and inefficient. After a brief encounter
with the Saracens, he decided to retreat. He had borrowed money for the crusade, he had failed to pay his
debts, and things were going badly in Hungary. Andrew went back home.

A fine king he was, said the castle gossips. Elizabeth
had come to the Wartburg a rich princess. Now her
father was in disgrace, and there was nothing for her
dowry. It was high time, said the Thuringian nobles,

that Elizabeth should be sent back to Hungary or put in a convent. They had been saying it more or less secretly for a long time. Now they did not hesitate to say it outright and to Elizabeth. Religion—that was all she seemed to think about anyway. Landgravine Sophie did not know what to say or do. Louis was away a good deal on state business, and even when he was at home, he did not like to listen to complaints about Elizabeth.

Louis was now preparing for the great day when he would become a knight. The date was set, and all the young nobles in the neighborhood were practicing for the tournament that was expected to take place on the eve of such a great event.

The ladies of the court were all in a pleasant stir of excitement, too. They spent a great deal of time with rose water and lemon juice to whiten their skins. They tried out new dance steps and practiced all their arts. Each one hoped that some handsome knight would claim her for his lady. For Louis there would be no lady but Elizabeth. The others all knew that, and for Elizabeth there was no knight but Louis. She made herself as beautiful as possible, hoping to be in some degree worthy of him.

For days the preparations went on. Tailors and sewing women were busy day and night. Quantities of food were prepared in the kitchens. The whole castle was scrubbed and polished. Then consternation!

"There will be no tournament", said Louis. "This is

a great and holy occasion. It is not suitable to celebrate such a day with swords and spears and warlike deeds. It should be a time of prayer."

The landgravine was displeased. The ladies sulked. The young men grumbled. They all blamed Elizabeth, but Louis had his way. He chose two of his most trusted friends to be his squires of honor, and he performed all the actions required of him with reverence and dignity. Before the night of his vigil he was examined by Walter of Varila and others of the most grave and reverend knights to show that he was well versed in all the rules of chivalry.

Louis kept his vigil in the church at Eisenach. Before he left the castle, however, he entered a large room hung with tapestries and embroidered linen. There he bathed in warm water, and his hair was cut in a special way. He put on a snow-white wool tunic to show that he was pure in heart, and over it a scarlet robe, meaning that he was ready to shed his blood for Holy Mother Church. A black coat over all reminded him that he must sometime die. When he was dressed, he and his squires rode down the dark path to the village.

While the people in the castle slept, Louis knelt before the tabernacle. On the step in front of him lay his armor, his sword, his shield, and his helmet. Between the tall white candles on the altar were vases of white flowers. Louis knew that Elizabeth had put them there, and his heart was filled with a holy love for his "little

Sister". He begged God to make him worthy to be her knight and champion. And while he prayed for her, Elizabeth, up in the castle, knelt beside her bed and kept the vigil, too. She prayed and prayed that she would never lose the love of her "dear Brother" and that she might be worthy of so true a knight.

As soon as the first light of dawn struck full upon the altar, Louis rose to begin the great day. One of his squires brought water in a silver basin with which to wash his face and hands. His first duty was confession and Holy Communion, after which he chanted Matins with the priests and monks who had come for the occasion and ate a frugal meal. Then the whole household came down from the castle for Mass.

Later in the day all the nobles gathered in the great vaulted hall hung with banners. Knights, ladies, and guests in elegant attire sat in the balconies. Plain citizens of Eisenach clad in sober russet and dun colors, archers and yeomen in green and brown, sat on benches along the sides. On special thrones sat the landgravine with Princess Agnes and Princess Elizabeth, who wore dresses of scarlet, embroidered with golden flowers and leaves. The dresses were of the greatest beauty, made especially for the knighting of Louis. No one but Guda knew that under all her finery Elizabeth wore a shirt of rough horsehair. On a raised platform covered with red satin, embroidered with lions and lilies, sat the archbishop with his attendants.

Suddenly there was a sound of trumpets, then a

silence, and a knight entered. He bore a fine sword in a red velvet scabbard, with golden spurs attached. Behind him came Louis, dressed all in white wool embroidered with silver. Over his new, polished armor he wore a tunic of white satin and silver. He did not look up at Elizabeth, and she was proud of his self-discipline.

The knight who carried the sword laid it on the knees of the archbishop, who blessed both sword and spurs. Then the knight knelt before Louis and fastened the spurs to his boots, making the Sign of the Cross as he did so. Next the archbishop unwound the belt from the scabbard. Everyone in the hall was silent.

Louis stepped forward, with an older knight on either side. The archbishop rose and adjusted the belt. Then, as Louis knelt before him, the archbishop struck him lightly on the shoulder with the sword.

"To the honor of God, I consecrate thee a knight", said the archbishop. "Be thou a good knight."

"I will," promised Louis. "I promise to be brave and honorable, to right the wrong, to maintain that which is good, to protect all women, to give help to those in trouble, and to show mercy to the weak and the defenseless."

When Louis finished speaking, loud cheers rang through the hall, and the whole court withdrew to the banquet hall, where a great feast had been prepared to do honor to the young prince on his great day. As he led Elizabeth to his place at the head of the table, Louis whispered, "I pledge my knighthood to God and to you, little Sister.

And Elizabeth answered, "God keep you always, my true and faithful knight!"

5

THE STORYTELLER SOWS THE SEED

"WHAT DO YOU SUPPOSE is going on?" whispered Guda anxiously to Isentrude, as they went about their daily tasks in the great assembly hall. "It looks like a family council."

"Poor Elizabeth!" answered Isentrude. "It bodes no good for her. There goes Agnes, looking very pleased with herself. Dame Bertha went in first with those two parrots, Ilse and Odilia! They echo every word Dame Bertha utters. All of them have been urging the landgravine to send Elizabeth home."

"I don't know why Odilia is so jealous", muttered Guda, keeping her back turned but not missing a thing for all that.

Something important was certainly going on in one of the private council rooms, for now two of the Wartburg knights appeared and stalked in after the ladies.

"They are the ones who said that Elizabeth couldn't be trusted with money or goods", said Isentrude softly. "They said she would endanger their own holdings by her extravagant ideas of charity."

In a moment or two Walter of Varila entered the council room, looking very grave, and last of all the landgravine appeared, with Louis at her side. Louis looked bewildered and disturbed. The door was closed, and Guda and Isentrude were left to their work and their unhappy thoughts.

Whatever went on behind that closed door, a change came over Louis. He spent most of his days in the saddle, hunting or riding out to oversee his farms and pastures. When he was in the castle, he stayed in the Knights' Hall and seemed purposely to avoid Elizabeth.

One day, Louis and some of his knights were returning from a tournament. Elizabeth, who had suffered much from his neglect, started running to meet him as usual. The landgravine pushed her back rather roughly, telling her that she had no business there. It was the first time that Elizabeth had to admit to herself that what she feared most was true. She was not to marry Louis! She was going to be sent home!

"Oh, dear God, don't take Louis away from me", prayed Elizabeth at the foot of the altar. For hours she lay there, weeping and begging God to give Louis back to her. It was almost as if she were struggling with God, her will against his. Exhausted at last, she gave up and raised her tear-stained face to the crucifix.

"Whatever you want, God, even if it means losing Louis."

Elizabeth's trial continued. Louis did not speak to her. He seemed not even to see her. He had brought her no present. At last he rode off with his knights without saying good-bye.

Elizabeth ran to the garden and hid herself in a corner where a tall hedge offered shelter. She did not see Walter of Varila pull his horse up beside that of his master. She did not hear what Varila said to Louis.

"My lord, may I ask a question?"

"Whatever you will, Varila."

"Then, my lord, may I ask what is your intention with regard to the Princess Elizabeth? You have always known that I promised her father on my honor as a knight to defend her. Is she to be sent back to Hungary?"

Louis was startled. He looked as if he had not until

that very moment realized what it would mean to lose Elizabeth.

"No, Varila, no! Elizabeth is dearer to me than anything else on earth. I will have no other for my bride."

"May I take this message to Elizabeth, my lord?"

"You may indeed, Varila, and take her this present to tell her that I love her."

Louis took from his pouch a beautiful little silver mirror, delicately made by a master silversmith, with the image of Christ wrought in filigree on the back. He gave it to Varila and rode away with a light heart for the first time in months. He had made an important decision. He would marry Elizabeth no matter what happened.

When Walter of Varila gave Elizabeth the long-awaited present, she threw herself into the arms of the kind old knight and cried herself out in relief and gladness. Elizabeth was twelve now, and girls of twelve were considered quite old enough for marriage. She had been well trained by the landgravine, and the court fully expected that the wedding would soon take place.

Even the worst of the court gossips gave up when they realized that Louis was determined to marry "the Hungarian", as they often spitefully called her. At once they began to pretend that they had always been friendly to Elizabeth. Even Agnes treated her more kindly. The landgravine was glad to have the question settled at last. She began to spend more time in the chapel herself, praying for the landgrave's soul.

But Louis had other decisions to make and other problems to solve. In spite of the fact that he was deeply religious, he felt bound to continue his father's fight to keep the clergy from seizing power and land from the nobles. He refused to surrender certain of his own lands to the archbishop of Mainz, who claimed them, and once more the Wartburg Castle fell under the ban of the Church. Louis was excommunicated.

This new blow fell heaviest on Elizabeth. Louis, her own knight, so good, so brave, so true, was cast out by the Church. He could not receive his Lord in Holy Communion. He could not be married, for marriage was one of the sacraments. Now the Wartburg Chapel, which had been reopened after the death of Landgrave Hermann, was empty. Again the tabernacle door stood open, and the darkness within struck the heart with fear and loneliness. No bell. No lights. No flowers. God had hidden his face again.

Louis gathered his followers and went forth to battle for his rights. He must force the archbishop of Mainz to free him from the excommunication ban before he could marry Elizabeth. For months he was away. Then one day Walter of Varila rode back to the castle with great news.

"The ban is lifted!" he shouted. "The ban is lifted!"

"Tell us quickly, Varila. How is Louis? Is he safe?"

Elizabeth caught at Varila's sleeve and watched him with anxious eyes.

"Prince Louis is safe and well. He has made peace

with the archbishop of Mainz, and the archbishop has agreed not only to lift the ban on Louis, but also to erase the blot on his father's memory."

"Thank God!" Everyone in the castle said the same thing. "Thank God! Thank God!"

All this happened in the year 1219, but it was nearly two years more before the wedding actually took place. The early thirteenth century was a difficult time for the rulers of kingdoms, and they were kept constantly on the go, defending what they possessed in lands, power, and money, and trying to get more. While Louis was gone, Landgravine Sophie continued to manage the castle and to train Elizabeth in the duties of a medieval lady whose husband would spend much of his time away from home.

Sometime during those two years of eager adventure, Louis met the young Emperor Frederick, whom he had always hoped to serve. Both the young men were devoted to the highest ideals of knighthood, and they became steadfast friends. Louis swore fealty to Frederick and vowed to serve him always. No doubt Louis knelt before Frederick as was the feudal custom, placed his folded hands between those of his friend and emperor, and made a solemn vow that he would follow Frederick and serve him unto death. It was Frederick, probably, who arranged the peace between Louis and the archbishop of Mainz.

Meanwhile, Elizabeth waited patiently. She prayed

and worked for Louis and looked forward with joy to those occasions when her knight came home for a brief visit. Louis never again failed to bring the expected present. He danced with Elizabeth, ate with her from the same plate in the banquet hall, prayed with her in the chapel—and was gone again.

Then suddenly, like a rainbow after a long storm, the wedding preparations began. All the color, excitement, and display that Louis would not permit at his knighting became a part of the wedding. The inns in Eisenach were jammed with guests. Every neighboring castle was full to the very turrets. Farmers fattened their geese. Pigs and calves were made ready for the feast, and cooks concocted the most remarkable pastries ever baked. Tailors, dressmakers, hairdressers, shoemakers, and armorers worked far into the night so that the nobles might have the finest raiment for the great occasion.

"Look at this tunic, Guda. Did you ever see anything so beautiful?"

"Is it for Louis, Elizabeth?"

"As if you didn't know!" Elizabeth laughed. "Dear Brother! Dear Brother! I am so happy, Guda!"

"I know, Elizabeth, I know!" Faithful Guda was happy, too.

Guda had already seen Elizabeth's wedding gown, beautiful enough for a fairy princess. It was made of white damask with silver embroidery, and there was a white velvet cloak of such weight and magnificence that Elizabeth sighed a little when she looked at it. She knew how heavy it would be on her shoulders.

There were dozens of other dresses and quantities of fine linen undergarments with delicate white embroidery and hundreds of tiny tucks. The women's apartment was strewn with ribbons and cloaks and veils. All the ladies were trying on jewelry and helping each other decide which ring or bracelet or earrings would be most effective.

For a whole week after the wedding there was feasting in the castle. Elizabeth had never been so happy. What more could God do for her? She had not been sent home, and here she was, actually dancing at her wedding to Louis. They made a beautiful picture—the tall, fair knight in his cloth of silver and the dark-haired little princess with the merry eyes, radiant in her lovely wedding gown. Everyone who saw them asked God to bless their marriage.

Elizabeth was only fourteen, but she was now the landgravine of Thuringia and the mistress of the Wartburg Castle. It was she who now presided over the banquets and festivals, wearing the fine Hungarian jewels that had been sent with her when she came in the silver cradle years before. She sat in state on the throne beside Louis to watch the tournaments and bestow prizes on the successful knights.

During the week's festivities, Henry and Conrad, the young brothers of Louis, were allowed to enter the lists for the first time, and Princess Agnes, fair and beautiful in cloth of gold, was formally introduced to the visiting nobles. Elizabeth, always generous and forgiving, forgot all the unkindness that Agnes had showed to her and treated her with love and sisterly pride.

"Well, now Elizabeth has settled down and forgotten all that childish foolishness about religion", said one of the ladies who had most often criticized her.

"She will be far too busy now to find time for long hours in the chapel", said another in a tone of satisfaction.

"I hope that Prince Louis will keep a firm hand on the purse strings if he doesn't want Elizabeth to give away most of his property, but I fear that he will be too easy with her."

"It is too bad that he will not have the landgravine to help him, but no doubt she is happier where she is."

After the wedding, Landgravine Sophie had written to Pope Honorius III. She was tired of court life and still greatly worried about her husband's eternal welfare. She was glad to turn the management of the castle over to the young people, but she wanted to retain control of her own property so that she could use it to pay back those who had been unjustly treated by her husband.

The landgravine asked the Pope's permission to remain a widow and to live with the Cistercian nuns of Saint Catherine in Eisenach as a lay nun. Many wealthy widows did so in those days. They followed the rule of the nuns with whom they lived, but they usually had their own private apartments and were free to come and go as they pleased. As soon as permission came from the Pope, the landgravine gave her blessing to Louis and Elizabeth and set out for Eisenach to begin her new life.

Now Louis and Elizabeth were free to rule the castle without interference. They were young and carefree and enjoyed entertaining their friends. One evening there was to be an especially brilliant banquet at the Wartburg, their first big party. Louis and Elizabeth held many a conference with the stewards, for they wanted only the finest foods and wines to be served. The cooks were ordered to make the most elaborate pastries and to search the markets for rare and unusual foods.

"What entertainment have you planned for the time before dancing begins?" asked Louis.

"Why, Louis, don't you remember? There is to be an important singing contest, and the pages have rehearsed a little play. Oh, yes, there is also a storyteller, a monk who came yesterday for alms and shelter. The servants say that he is quite remarkable. He entertained them for hours last night."

"A monk, Elizabeth?"

"Yes. His name is Brother Andrew, and he calls himself a Gray Brother."

Louis looked as if he were about to say something. Then he laughed. He put his finger under Elizabeth's chin and lifted her head, which had drooped when she thought Louis was displeased.

"So you have already asked the Gray Brother. Well, he will certainly be an innovation, almost more astonishing than the stuffed peacocks, to be served with tails outspread, that Emil is preparing in the kitchen. Come, smile again, little Sister. This will be a memorable banquet."

And it was. There was a great procession of knights and ladies into the banquet hall. Louis and Elizabeth entered last and took their places at the master's table at one end of the room. Agnes was already in her place. The younger boys, Henry and Conrad, were serving as pages to neighboring knights. Torches flared, violins played softly in the minstrels' gallery, and pages hurried about, bearing flagons of wine and great platters of smoking food. The astonishing stuffed peacocks, with huge blue tails outspread showing a hundred jeweled eyes, drew exclamations of surprise and pleasure.

When the guests had all well feasted and were beginning to quiet down, as those will who have eaten more than is good for them, the master minstrel gave a sign. In the large open space between the tables the pages staged their play. Some of the boys, wearing borrowed garments, played ladies and earned much laughter and applause for their little dramatic sketch about a runaway couple and an angry father.

After the play came the singing contest, in which two master singers competed for a prize. They were men who had made a career of singing and were so nearly matched in skill that the guests found it difficult to decide. The prize was finally awarded to the older of the two, who had sung a stirring ballad of the bygone days in Germany and the heroic deeds of a legendary knight.

When the applause had subsided and the audience was once again quiet, the master minstrel signaled to the Gray Brother. He had humbly insisted upon sitting far down at the end of the table with the least important people. Now he came forward in his rough gray habit, which had a hood at the back and a heavy cord around the waist.

Some of the guests looked amused or puzzled, but most of them were impressed by the deep dark eyes of the Gray Brother and the beautiful voice in which he began to speak. He was a born storyteller, there was no doubt of that. He told ancient stories from German folklore and hero tales from history. Then he began to talk of something quite different. He told of a man in Italy whose name was Francis Bernardone, a cheery, extravagant, and very popular young nobleman of Assisi, the son of a wealthy cloth merchant.

"Every night," said Brother Andrew, "young Francis and his friends roamed the streets of Assisi, stopping to eat and drink at every tavern, playing their lutes and viols, and waking the sleeping people with their noisy chatter."

The storyteller recounted how Signor Bernardone

scolded Francis because his son had no regard for money and had even sold rolls of cloth from the shop to get money to give to the poor.

"But Francis was not satisfied with the life he led", went on the Gray Brother. "One day he came upon a crucifix in an abandoned chapel in the woods. There he prayed fervently, and suddenly he saw a vision of our Lord and Savior, Jesus Christ, upon the cross, so close and alive that the heart of Francis almost stood still. 'Go hence, Francis', Christ said to him gently. 'Go hence and build up my house. It is falling down.' Then Francis understood that Christ wanted him to restore the whole Christian Church, which is decaying because people care more now for wealth and power and entertainment than they do for their immortal souls."

By now the flame of the torches was dying. Shadows lay deep in the corners of the hall and fell upon the faces of the knights and ladies who had been listening attentively. Elizabeth was leaning forward, her eyes fixed on the speaker. She did not move at all.

"Francis now knew what he must do", continued Brother Andrew. "He changed his rich clothing for a rough gray garment with a rope for a girdle and began to beg his food from door to door. He had always been repelled by dirt and disorder and had hated the look and the smell of sickness and poverty.

"Now he forced himself to go to the leper colony. As the lepers crowded around him, blind or deformed, with ugly sores and the terrible odor of leprosy, Francis kissed their hands as he gave each one an alms. Only God knew what an effort of the will it took. Nothing would ever be so hard again."

Brother Andrew paused a moment. Then he raised his voice.

"Then Francis gathered around him other young men who joined him in a life of poverty and penance. I am one of them. We wear gray garments, too, as you see, with rope girdles and sandals on our feet. We make little shelters of branches and eat what scraps we can beg. Two by two we go about the country preaching the gospel and begging the people to repent of their sins and turn to Christ."

The speaker, noting that his audience was growing a little restless now that his stories had turned into a sermon, hurried to a conclusion. He told how the Gray Brothers began to call themselves Franciscans, how many among them became priests, forming the First Order, and how a Second Order of nuns had been formed, with a young noblewoman, Clare of Assisi, the first to join. He ended with a plea that his hearers receive the Gray Brothers whom Brother Francis would soon send to their country. He hoped that there might be many to join them in poverty and humility, praying with Brother Francis the prayer that he taught them:

"We adore thee, most holy Lord Jesus Christ, and we bless thee, because by thy holy cross thou hast redeemed the world."

Then fresh torches were brought, the music began for dancing, and Elizabeth resumed her duties as hostess. But she was deeply touched by the words of the Gray Brother. The seed that he sowed in her heart that night was to flower into an intense desire to become a follower of Francis of Assisi and to help him rebuild God's house.

6

MISTRESS OF WARTBURG

A LOUD CLAP of thunder! A zigzag of lightning across the sky!

"Turn your horse back, Elizabeth. We can get home before the storm breaks if we hurry."

"No, no! Follow me, Louis", Elizabeth called back over her shoulder. "I'm not afraid of thunder. I love to ride in the rain."

Elizabeth felt so alive that she didn't know how to express the feeling. She loved being mistress of the Wartburg Castle and ruler of so many people. She loved Louis so much that she couldn't bear to be away from him even for a little while. Sometimes she was afraid that she put Louis before God. Then she was frightened. She fell on her knees and begged God to keep her close to him and to bless her love for Louis.

The Wartburg Castle rang again with happiness and excitement as it had done in the times when Landgrave Hermann was the master. The days were filled with tournaments, visits, and hunting parties, and every evening there was entertainment of some kind in the great hall. In the minstrels' gallery musicians played for dancing. Lutes, harps, and violins played sweet music, and when the party grew merrier, the bagpipes sounded a sharper note and the drummers rattled on the tabors.

Although there were jugglers, acrobats, and tumblers to look at, and minstrels, poets, and gleemen to listen to, for entertainment the knights and their ladies liked dancing best. It gave the women a chance to display their clothes and their jewels and the knights a chance to show off their ladies. Louis could well be proud of Elizabeth now. There was no one more brilliant or more lavishly dressed. She could dance half the night without tiring—but not even Louis knew of the hair shirt she wore under her gold brocade.

Louis still brought presents to Elizabeth. She was especially fond of a silver whistle he had given her to call back her falcon after a flight. She loved to gallop along with the other hunters, to unhood and release her beautiful white falcon, and to watch him mount and drop straight down upon his prey. Then she would blow her little silver whistle and back would come the well-trained bird to his place on her gloved wrist while the dogs retrieved the game. It was an exciting sport, and Elizabeth loved it.

Now that Louis and Elizabeth were rulers of the great, rambling Wartburg Castle, they looked at it with a new interest. The Wartburg was more than a hundred years old even then, and one of the more beautiful of the medieval castles. It had looked dark and grim to little four-year-old Elizabeth, but now at fourteen she knew enough to appreciate the lovely arched gateway, the rows of arched windows, and the high tower where she and Louis often stood and looked down with pride at the miles of mountains and forest that belonged to them.

The castle was huge. The people of the Middle Ages needed strong legs to carry them up the narrow, winding steps to the terraces and towers or down to the cisterns and the dungeons. The stables housed great numbers of Spanish, Hungarian, and Arabian saddle horses, as well as other fine, intelligent steeds trained for battle, and strong work horses for the farms and heavy labor. There were rough quarters for the grooms and hostlers and barracks for the men-at-arms who might at any moment have to defend the castle from attack.

Some walls of the castle were eight feet thick, built to withstand assault during a long siege. Down at the lowest level were the cellars and storerooms. Narrow passages crisscrossed each other. Hidden stairways and secret tunnels led to the moat and a chance of escape in danger. Outside in the courtyards were stored scaling ladders, movable towers on rollers, battering rams, catapults, and all the other instruments of war.

As Louis and Elizabeth went over the castle hand in hand, they talked of improvements to be made and places where repairs would be necessary.

"We need a larger banquet hall", said Louis one day. "We must entertain hundreds here at the next tournament, and our hall is not large enough. We are always too crowded. What do you think, Elizabeth?"

"Oh, we do indeed need a larger hall, Louis. Let us build a glorious big one the whole length and breadth of the first floor."

"Well, I was not thinking of anything as big as that —but why not?"

"With a raised platform across one end and a great carved table and chairs for our family and special guests", went on Elizabeth. Already she had the whole thing planned in her mind—the stained-glass windows, the rich paintings on the walls, and the many-colored banners hanging from the carved and painted rafters. She could see the heavy gold platters, the tall silver candlesticks, and the long procession of squires and pages carrying smoking pastries of chicken, pigeon, grouse, and partridge. She would have the most beautiful festival hall in Europe.

What about the kitchen? Down they went into the great vaulted room where the head cook and his scores of assistants labored all day to prepare the vast quantities of food that went upstairs to the feasting nobles. The head cook carried an enormous wooden spoon. That was his badge of office. He used it frequently, too, to hasten lagging footsteps or to punish a clumsy scullion.

Great ovens were ranged on one side. There was a tremendous open fireplace, big enough to roast a whole ox or a deer. On the walls hung copper cauldrons, ladles, strainers, graters, and saucepans. On long, solid oak tables the servants prepared soups and stews; meat, fish, and game dishes; sauces and desserts.

"We must explain to the head cook about the pepper", said Elizabeth. "He used so much on the venison last night that the guests drank twice as much wine as usual."

"So the steward reports", replied Louis. "I noticed myself that the pepper made me very thirsty. It is so new to us that everyone needs time to get used to it."

Louis had planted vineyards on many sunny slopes and was gaining a fine income from the sale of wine. He served his finest wines on his own banquet tables, and many a cask was opened after pepper became commonly used in cooking. All the meat dishes were very heavily spiced, but pepper made people thirsty and sometimes caused them to choke and cough. The good wine from the Wartburg vineyards sent a cool and pleasant trickle down their throats.

Sometimes Elizabeth persuaded Louis to ride with her alone down into the village and along the country roads. They clothed themselves in the plainest of garments and wore no sign of rank. They stopped at humble one-room homes and talked with the people, noting the straw thatch, the smoky fire for heat and cooking right in the middle of the dirt floor, and the animals housed under the same roof.

Elizabeth was better at this sort of thing than Louis. She played with the children and asked questions of the villagers. And she was very much shocked to learn what the peasants really thought about the "people up there", by which they meant the nobles who lived up in the Wartburg. Whenever Elizabeth had ridden down to the church in Eisenach, the people had cheered and waved at the nobles, and the nobles had bowed and smiled. Now she knew what they really thought and how they hated the people who grew rich as a result of their misery. They told her disturbing stories of hard work, heavy taxes, and cruel treatment by the bailiffs who had to collect the money from the peasants to support the nobles in luxury.

The rich people were getting richer, and the peasants poorer. The nobles continued to go to Mass and to practice the outward forms of religion, but they were not truly charitable. Elizabeth could see that. She felt more and more that she must give herself as Christ did, as Brother Francis did. If the people were to serve God better, someone must show the way.

At this point, Elizabeth was living a kind of divided life. She was trying to find some way to serve God and Louis, too. She was trying to live *in* the world as if she were not *of* the world—and it was far from easy.

There was a great deal of visiting back and forth among the ladies of the various castles near the Wartburg, and after the first excitement of the wedding was over, court gossip began to run riot again.

"I never know what to do when she is visiting me", complained one of the ladies as she admired her parrot in his golden cage. "Everyone says that she dislikes ceremony and display. Still, she *is* the landgravine, and it is proper to show her honor by using our finest things."

"She is very disappointing", remarked another, looking up from the design that she was painting on parchment. "She is supposed to set the fashions and send messengers to find out what is being worn in Paris, but when she is in one of her pious moods, I don't believe she knows *what* she is wearing. She would probably wear sackcloth and ashes to a banquet if she dared!"

Another lady spoke. She had been reading her Psalter and looked quite serious.

"Sometimes I think she is right. She is very kind and considerate, and she has given me good advice. She does things for the sick and poor that none of us would do."

"Ugh! I should think not. How can she touch those dirty beggars and wash their sores? Why doesn't she send a servant? She goes down to Eisenach and cleans out their miserable houses and nurses people who have the plague. And she laughs and sings while she's doing it!"

"Did you see her that night at the banquet when that monk was telling about the Gray Brothers who have just come to Germany? Some Brother Francis sent them from Italy. She never took her eyes from his face. You would think she was in a trance. I always said she should have been a nun."

But none of the ladies of the court knew even half of the things Elizabeth was doing for the love of God. The stories she continued to hear about the Gray Brothers made a tremendous impression on her. It was true that she sang happily while performing the most loathsome tasks, but, like Brother Francis, she had to teach herself to overcome fear, cold, fatigue, and a natural dislike of disease and ugliness.

Elizabeth took Guda and Isentrude with her on her errands of mercy. At first they grumbled a good deal, but after a while they caught some of her spirit of charity and went willingly.

"Jesus Christ has sent me!" Elizabeth told the grateful and wondering peasants. They could not believe that a princess would come to their wretched huts and serve them personally.

One day Elizabeth ordered Guda and Isentrude to wait at a certain place while she went all by herself to a nearby leper village. She was a little breathless, a good deal frightened, and fearful of what Louis would think this time. The lepers were in great fear when they saw her coming and sounded their rattles as loudly as they could to hold her back, but she kept right on toward them.

"God greet you!" said Elizabeth. She felt sick at the sights and the smells, but she thought of how Christ had healed the lepers. She sat on a stone bench nearby, and the wondering lepers knelt near her.

"I am come from Jesus Christ", she said. Then she told the lepers about Christ, who had died for them. In his name she gave her gifts of food, clothing, and money, but her greatest gift was her victory over herself. Both Elizabeth and Brother Francis felt the most intense loathing for everything connected with leprosy, but, for the love of God, they overcame their human weakness.

One of the problems that Elizabeth had to solve was to find sufficient time for prayer. She knew that good works were important, but she also knew that she could not please God and save her soul by works of charity alone. She must pray.

Although she and Louis heard Mass every day together, the rest of her day was so full of her duties as landgravine that the only way she could find time for prayer was by stealing it from her hours of rest. She would go to bed at the proper time, but she would make Guda or Isentrude wake her after an hour or two. Then she would kneel on the cold floor at the side of the great canopied four-poster bed with its heavy curtains and pray for hours.

Louis often pretended to be asleep, but he knew well enough what Elizabeth was doing, and he was very anxious about her health. Often he would reach out to find her cold hands clasped on the side of the bed, and he would cover them with his warm ones.

"Spare yourself, little Sister", he would say gently. But he did not interfere with her devotions. It may be that God had made known to him in some way that this dear young wife of his would someday be a saint.

Many legends have grown up around Elizabeth. One day, it is said, having given away everything else, she gave a poor beggar one of her jeweled gloves. A young knight gave the beggar a goodly sum for the glove, which he placed on his helmet, hoping for divine protection. Already, it seems, the people were beginning to think of Elizabeth as a saint.

Another time, when she had given away all her clothes but a rough woolen garment, Louis rode home with important guests. Louis was really troubled when he saw her coming to greet them, but by the time she had reached the company she was arrayed in a magnificent gown and wore her jeweled crown. Guda and Isentrude were used to miracles where Elizabeth was concerned, but even they were astonished at the way God protected her on this occasion.

A favorite story, which has also been told of other saints, concerns the time that Louis met her when she was carrying a great basketful of food and garments to the poor. The story has it that Louis spoke to her angrily and asked her what she was hiding under her cloak. When he pulled the cloak aside, the basket was full of roses! The story does not ring true for Louis and Elizabeth, because he never scolded, no matter how much she gave away.

Agnes was always quick to report to her brother tales of Elizabeth's lavish giving and unseemly behavior. The stewards and bailiffs and even some of the vassals sometimes objected, too, but Louis defended her, no matter who complained or criticized.

It is no wonder that the German people always had a great affection for Louis. He was considered to be one of the best and ablest men of his time. In spite of quarrels with the Church over property rights, he was a truly good man. The people who knew him, both nobles and peasants, held him in great affection, and there were many who called him a saint.

7

A VISIT HOME

"HEAR THE BELLS, Elizabeth! They are ringing
for you. Does the road look familiar now?"

"Not all of it. I remember that carved wooden
bridge over the Danube. When I was very small, the
river used to look like a silver ribbon looped around
the castle. Look, Louis! They are throwing flower pet-
als in our path. It is so good to be coming home!"

Elizabeth and Louis were riding up the mountain to the mighty Pressburg Castle with its four square towers, the castle that Elizabeth had left in a silver cradle more than ten years before. It was her first visit to Hungary in all those years, and she was returning with a magnificent procession of knights and vassals as landgravine of Thuringia and the wife of the most powerful ruler in all Germany. Everyone in the village was in the streets to greet the royal pair, waving flags, scattering flowers, and calling out greetings and congratulations.

There was no mother to greet Elizabeth, but King Andrew had sent a company of knights in golden armor to meet them. The knights lined up opposite each other and raised their swords with points touching to make an archway for Elizabeth and Louis to ride under. The king himself held out welcoming arms at the gate of the castle. He asked if Varila had come and was greatly pleased when that good knight stepped forward.

From all over the kingdom Hungarians gathered, proud and happy to have their princess back home for a visit. They made speeches and sent scrolls of welcome and rich gifts for Louis as well as for Elizabeth. It delighted her to hear again the language of her childhood. Old servants who remembered her came to kiss her hands and the hem of her garments. Once more she heard the gypsy fiddles play the *czardas* and rode out into the golden sunshine with her father's knights.

Elizabeth had brought Guda and watched with joy her faithful friend's meeting with her mother.

Every day at the castle there were dancing, hunting, drives to neighboring fairs, and the clash of arms at brilliant tournaments. All kinds of new and delicious foods were served, and the roasted meats were spiced with cinnamon, cloves, and nutmeg, as well as pepper. Sweet wines were served in slender goblets, and bowls of fruit were heaped so high that golden oranges and rosy peaches dropped from their places and rolled unheeded across the bright tiled floor.

Elizabeth had heard so many tales of her father's poverty, his disloyalty, and his lack of courage that she was glad indeed to find his court as rich and splendid as ever. It gave her great satisfaction to have the German vassals who had come with them see what a magnificent castle the Pressburg was and exclaim over the marvelous gifts showered upon them by her father.

Another thing that gave comfort to Elizabeth and answered questions that had troubled her for many years was the report she now heard concerning her mother's death. Back in the Wartburg nothing had been said in favor of Queen Gertrude. Now Elizabeth learned that the Hungarian people were actually devoted to her mother's memory. They said that the queen had defied the murderers and saved King Andrew's life at the expense of her own. Elizabeth's heart, which had always been heavy at the thought of her mother, was much lighter when the Germans who had come with her joined the Hungarian nobles and went to the chapel in the Pressburg to pray for her mother's soul.

After the first excitement of seeing her father and her own country again, Elizabeth began to think of all the grandeur of her father's court. She recalled the vast sums spent on the gorgeous clothes that she and Louis had brought with them, and the gifts they had lavished on the Hungarian court. But what of the poor? What of the people who were so cruelly taxed to provide these things? What did God think of this journey? Was he displeased and disappointed? Elizabeth and Louis talked about it far into the night. What was happening to the world? What had become of the old spirit of the crusades? Most of the rulers thought only of their crowns, their lands, their property. They were greedy for power and money.

Elizabeth was filled with shame and sorrow. She felt that the Christian rulers had betrayed Christ.

"Dear Louis, I wish we were poor!"

"Poor?"

"Yes, really poor. I should like to sell everything we possess—the Wartburg and everything in it—and give all we get to the poor. We could buy a little cottage with a few acres of land. You could have a pair of horses to plow the land, and I would keep a flock of sheep."

"But dear, dear little Sister, we can't do that. A ruler has to lead his people. They would not obey him or respect him if he were just like themselves."

Elizabeth gave up. She knew that she could not persuade Louis that it was right for a Christian king to be poor. She was sorry, too, for all the anxiety she must constantly cause him. No other knight in all Christendom would be so patient. He would not scold or interfere with her in her search for holiness, but he himself had quite a different opinion of the obligations of a ruler and the meaning of knighthood. Well, if she could not give up all her worldly possessions, she would have to give more of herself. There was no other way.

It was not long after her return to Thuringia that God sent help to Elizabeth. A large band of Gray Brothers arrived in Germany with a letter from Brother Francis. It was read in churches, chapels, and convents, and Elizabeth received it with joy as a long-awaited message from God himself.

Francis made an urgent appeal to all Christians to praise God and avoid sin, to practice obedience and mutual charity, and to cast all care for the concerns of body and soul upon the Good Shepherd, our Lord Jesus Christ. He encouraged them to observe patience in adversity, humility and mildness, and a burning zeal for holy charity.

Soon the friars appeared in Eisenach. They had started a small community not far away and were preaching throughout the countryside. The first one to enter the Wartburg Castle was Brother Rodiger. His arrival was a fateful moment for the young landgravine. Never did a preacher have a more eager listener. It seemed to Elizabeth that everything the friar said was an answer to prayer. Now, indeed, God was telling her what to do. The good friar became her spiritual adviser, and Elizabeth began quite definitely her step-by-step climb toward sainthood.

The Gray Brothers, who were also called Minor Brothers because Brother Francis so loved humility, had no chapel of their own, so Elizabeth had one built for them. Brother Rodiger was deeply impressed by Elizabeth's spirit of poverty and charity. He felt her to be already so holy that he almost feared to direct her, lest he hinder, rather than help, her in seeking perfection.

Some of the old records claim that the Minor Brothers told Brother Francis about Elizabeth and that he sent her his own cloak in gratitude for her help to the friars. The same writers say that she always wore the cloak when she wanted a special favor or was in need of direction. Certainly she became more intensely aware of Christ as her Savior and often spent long hours in the chapel weeping over her sins and the sins of the world. So closely united with Christ did she seem to be at such times that no one dared to disturb her. People in those days had never heard of daily Communion. Even nuns did not receive more than a few times a year. When Elizabeth did receive, however, priests often noticed that her face was transfigured and shone as if there were a candle lighted within.

" 'Leave everything and follow me' ", said Brother Rodiger. "Do you believe that Christ really meant those words?"

"Oh, I do believe," said Elizabeth, "I do believe. But I am not strong enough. I am too attached to my home and to my husband. I would like to be free as a bird and fly straight to heaven, but I am tied to earth with strong bonds. What can I do, Brother Rodiger?"

"Everyone must go his own way to heaven", said Brother Rodiger. "God speaks differently to every soul. But you must follow the voice of God, no matter what others say or do. Your duty to God comes first, even to giving up home and family. I will pray for you, Elizabeth."

"Lord Jesus, set free the soul of our sister Elizabeth", prayed Brother Rodiger. He felt sure that God was calling her to be a saint, but he feared the ties that held her to the usual life of a medieval princess. He even feared for his own soul in the midst of all the luxury, so he lived in the servants' quarters and ate his bread and water and a few green leafy vegetables out in the courtyard. Elizabeth wanted to do the same thing, but she knew how much the whole household would be offended. She was not ready yet.

A touching little story is told about Elizabeth as she was at this time of her life. Like so many other stories, it involves a beautiful cloak or mantle. Louis was giving a splendid banquet to show off the wonderful presents from Hungary. The guests were all assembled. No Elizabeth. She was on her way, indeed, but on the stairs lay a ragged, moaning beggar. How he got in, nobody knew. Elizabeth stopped on the stairs. She was already late. For a minute she gave way to natural annoyance. Then she remembered Brother Rodiger and made up her mind in a second. She tore the heavy cloak from her shoulders and gave it to the beggar. Now she could not enter the banquet hall. To do so without her mantle would be unthinkable. What could she do?

The Lord High Steward came angrily to Louis. "Our noble mistress has given away her costly cloak—the only one she had left—and she cannot appear before her guests."

Louis laughed. He knew his wife by this time. Up the steps he went to find her. "Where is your mantle, dear Sister? Our guests are waiting."

"On the rack", she said, looking up at him miserably. God had helped her before so that she wouldn't shame Louis.

"Bring your lady's mantle", said Louis to poor Guda, always at Elizabeth's side.

Guda returned immediately with a most beautiful cloak. It was right where Elizabeth had said it was, but it was not the one she had intended to wear. This one was the blue of our Lady, embroidered with small images of gold. After Elizabeth died, it was used as a vestment in the Franciscan monastery in Eisenach.

Louis was away all winter. He was a good ruler and went constantly among his people, holding councils and enforcing law and order throughout the kingdom. Whenever he rode forth, Elizabeth watched the knights galloping out over the drawbridge. They wore all kinds of devices on their shields, such as green crosses, blue wolves, dragons, and black bears. She could always tell which was Louis, even at a distance. Over his armor he wore a loose red mantle embroidered with golden lions, and his war horse was caparisoned in the same material.

All the long winter Elizabeth watched and prayed for Louis, but he did not come. Then, on March 28, in the year 1222, her first child was born in the Kreuzburg, one of the many castles belonging to Louis. Elizabeth was just fifteen. She was happy beyond words that she had a son to offer to Louis when he finally returned. He was on his way home when a messenger came riding like the wind to tell him that he had a son. The old records say that he was "inexpressibly glad, and all those with him rejoiced and praised God".

The small son of Louis and Elizabeth was named Hermann, after his grandfather. Elizabeth offered him to God and prayed for his blessing on the child. Louis held the baby clumsily in his great warrior's hands and thought only, "I must make ready an empire for him."

On the day that the landgrave and his wife and son returned to the Wartburg, there was great rejoicing. As the golden coach rolled through the village and climbed the hill, everyone tried to catch a glimpse of the new heir. Flowers were tossed into the coach, bells pealed, trumpets sounded, and the people shouted, "Long live the landgrave! Long live the landgravine! Long live Prince Hermann!"

When the Christ-child was born, the Blessed Virgin went up to the temple in Jerusalem with two turtle doves as her offering and gave thanks, just like ordinary mothers. Elizabeth wanted to be like the Blessed Virgin. She put on a simple woolen dress and walked barefoot down the steep path to Saint Catherine's, carrying her baby in her arms. Guda carried a lamb, and Isentrude a tall white candle. Elizabeth's feet were soon bruised, bleeding, and cold from the deep snow, but she was so happy that she hardly noticed.

It was Vesper time, and the nuns were chanting the evening prayer. No one paid any attention to the three young women in the dark dresses. They did not know that one of them was their own landgravine, nor that they were looking at one who would become a saint.

Some time later, the baby was baptized at Saint Catherine's. He wore a long white robe of the finest handmade lace and a hooded cape of embroidered white satin. Louis and Elizabeth were filled with love and pride, but Elizabeth felt a little tug at her heart. Would the baby keep her from God? She had nurses and servants in plenty, but did God want her to care for the baby herself? This tiny human being held her to earth with the strongest kind of ties.

Elizabeth's old silver cradle now became the resting place of her sturdy little son. But while he was growing and laughing and making the small strange sounds that babies make, his father, the landgrave, was riding far away in the service of the emperor. Elizabeth was restless.

"What shall I do, Brother Rodiger?"

The good friar shook his head.

"God will tell you what to do, Elizabeth. Your duty now is to your son."

"I wish I were strong enough to give up everything —to leave Louis and the baby and go to the nuns in Eisenach. When Louis is away, I pray and pray, and I think that God wants me to go. But as soon as Louis returns, I know that I cannot leave him. What shall I do, Brother Rodiger? My will is too weak to do the will of God."

"It pleases God, Elizabeth," said Brother Rodiger, "if each person practices virtue according to his station in life. You are a ruler, a wife, and a mother. It is very difficult, but not impossible, to practice poverty as a wealthy ruler, but you can practice other virtues, such as patience, humility, and charity, as you now do. Your own will is to give up everything. It may be God's will for you to remain as you are. Your greatest offering would be to give up your own will."

"But how shall I know, Brother Rodiger? How shall I know?"

"Pray, Elizabeth, pray!"

Brother Rodiger continued to urge her to pray for light, and he himself prayed constantly:

"Lord Jesus, set free the soul of our sister Elizabeth."

So Elizabeth prayed, but she did more than that. She followed the teachings of Brother Francis as she had heard them from the Gray Brothers, and her chief concern was for the unfortunate lepers.

A particularly touching story is told of her at this period. In spite of law and social custom, Elizabeth not only visited the lepers, but she encouraged them to come to the castle for help. One night Louis came home late, tired from a long day in the saddle. When he pulled back the curtain of his bed, there was a leper! Saints must certainly be difficult people to live with, and Louis might well have been excused had he lost his temper, but he didn't.

The Landgravine Sophie was visiting in the castle. She and Agnes followed Louis, complaining angrily that Elizabeth should dare to put a leper in her husband's bed. Louis, however, stood rooted to the spot, for suddenly the leper's face became the face of Christ. Louis fell to his knees.

"Elizabeth, dear Sister," he said, "it is Christ whom you have bathed and fed and cared for. Let us both do what we can to serve him by serving his suffering poor."

So the days passed for Elizabeth with penance, vigils, and almsgiving, as well as the daily duties and ceremonies of the castle. During one of his absences Louis was taken ill with fever and cared for by the good monks of a nearby monastery. Elizabeth didn't know about it until he came home, but fear clutched at her heart even when she knew that he was well again. He brought her a lovely white shell from the sea. Dear Louis! He never forgot the little presents.

On May 24, 1224, Elizabeth's second child was born, a little girl who was named Sophie, for her grandmother. Elizabeth was now seventeen. In token of his joy and gratitude, Louis had a handsome stone bridge built over the river, but Elizabeth had not yet found the bridge she sought—the bridge that led to complete surrender.

8

FASTING, FAMINE, AND THE PLAGUE

"Have you seen Master Conrad?"

"No, do tell us about him. What is he like?"

"Oh, they say he is a most scholarly man and that he is just and holy, too—but he frightens me."

"Is he as severe as everyone says he is?"

"Yes, indeed. He speaks very sternly, and he never smiles. I am surprised that the landgrave would bring such a person into the castle as a spiritual director for the landgravine. She is already pious enough. There's no telling what he will make her do!"

"Are all of us expected to obey him?"

"No, just the landgravine, I believe. But he is to preach in the chapel here, and she will see to it that we are all there!"

The ladies of the court were in a state of great excitement over the newcomer to the castle. From the beginning they did not like him, and they feared his influence on Elizabeth. With the exception of Guda and Isentrude and one or two others, the women who lived in the castle and knew Elizabeth well never seemed to realize what an extraordinary person she was. They were more concerned with the inconvenience she caused them than with the sanctity that Louis recognized in his young wife.

Louis believed more and more that Elizabeth was actually a saint in the making. He loved her so much and felt so responsible for the beautiful soul entrusted to him that he felt obliged to find someone to guide her, some good priest who would see how holy she was and who could help her become even holier.

Brother Rodiger had left the Wartburg to join the Franciscans in another town. Before he left, a strange thing happened. One day, while he was talking to Elizabeth and her companions, she was complaining because God permitted her to have so many distractions when she wanted to think of nothing but him.

A tree stood on the opposite bank of a little stream, and Brother Rodiger pointed to it. "That tree could cross the stream more easily than God could cease returning the love of his creatures", said the good Gray Brother.

Suddenly, the tree began to move. It crossed the stream and put its roots down into the ground before them. Elizabeth fell to her knees and asked pardon of God and of Brother Rodiger, too.

Louis had seen so many of these miracles by now that he felt a little frightened. He didn't know how to help Elizabeth himself, so he went to the highest authority he knew. He wrote to the Pope. He asked Pope Honorius to recommend a pious and learned teacher for his young wife, the Landgravine Elizabeth.

It happened that, just at the time Louis wrote, a man who was considered one of the wisest and holiest priests in all Germany was traveling throughout the country, fasting, preaching, and riding on a mule in a spirit of poverty. He was harsh and severe with himself and with others and, in nearly all respects, very unlike the gentle Franciscans. This man was known as Master Conrad of Marburg, and it was he whom Pope Honorius sent to direct the soul of the young landgravine.

Elizabeth was very happy when she heard that Master Conrad was coming. She thanked God humbly for his mercy in sending her a teacher. When she saw him for the first time, however, she was frightened.

Elizabeth knelt before her new spiritual adviser. She was only eighteen. "Good Father," she said, "I am unworthy to have you as my teacher, but I will do whatever you say."

Master Conrad made it known after Elizabeth's death that it was given to him at that moment to see this soul that was entrusted to him. It was shining with such a radiance that he gave thanks to God and begged for light to direct her.

It is doubtful that Louis had any idea of the great strictness with which Master Conrad would treat Elizabeth, of the extreme penances that he would urge upon her, or of the exact obedience he would demand. Louis may even have felt that a good, wise teacher might restrain her somewhat from her own excesses. But whatever Louis had in mind, from the moment Master Conrad arrived at the Wartburg he exercised complete control over Elizabeth.

One thing is certain. Elizabeth deliberately chose to obey Master Conrad. She always made herself do everything she was afraid to do or disliked to do—and she was afraid of Conrad.

"If I can have such fear of a mortal man, how much more must I fear almighty God, the Lord and Judge of all", she said to Guda.

Another thing is certain. Louis permitted her to undertake many courses of action even when he did not approve. He never failed her. So it was that Elizabeth went down to the church in Eisenach to pledge eternal obedience to Master Conrad of Marburg. She asked Louis to come with her and to bring the children. She also persuaded Guda and Isentrude and a third friend, named Ermingard, to take the vow with her. Elizabeth was now irrevocably pledged to God.

Master Conrad was a harsh teacher, but there must be someone to try the souls of the saints, as gold is tried in the furnace. Those who are chosen by God for their unwelcome task are often as much misunderstood as those whose souls are placed in their care.

Master Conrad made Elizabeth keep severe fasts and laid down laws that were nearly impossible to follow. She must eat nothing that might have come from unjust peasant labor or was grown on land that Louis might have taken from someone else by force.

How could Elizabeth know whether a pheasant or duck was shot on land that belonged without doubt to Louis? How could she be sure that the grain from which a certain loaf of bread was made came from fields that were certainly the property of the Wartburg? Anyone who lived in the Middle Ages would laugh at the idea. But Elizabeth tried her best and went hungry when she could not be sure.

Since the young landgravine had money of her own, she began to buy food from the nobility of other castles so that her companions, at least, might eat. She was distressed, not for herself, but for them. When Master Conrad heard of it, however, he was very angry. How could she be sure of that food, either? She must never do such a thing again! Never! So the poor girls were often very hungry.

In spite of the great severity of the life she was now leading, Elizabeth was as happy as a child when she thought that she was making even a little progress in holiness.

"Am I growing even a little more like what God wants me to be?" she would ask, and if Master Conrad said yes, as he occasionally did, her face lit up with childlike joy.

It was this very childlikeness that Master Conrad tried to suppress. Elizabeth had always been cheerful and friendly. Now she was punished for what, to most people, would seem to be her most attractive characteristic. One day, for a small infraction of the rules for which she was not really to blame anyway, he announced that he was leaving. Since she did not obey absolutely, she was not keeping her vow. There was no point in his remaining. He would leave.

Elizabeth's heart sank. If Master Conrad were going to leave, then God must have abandoned her. He must have decided that she was not fit for heaven, that she was not worth bothering with. She threw herself at Master Conrad's feet and begged him to remain. So did Guda and Isentrude. At last he forgave Elizabeth and agreed to remain, but he imposed on her an unusually severe penance.

In the winter of 1225–26, Elizabeth did not need to look far for penance and mortification even more severe than any imposed by Master Conrad. Earlier in the year Princess Agnes of Thuringia, the sister of Louis, was married with great ceremony to Prince Heinrich of Austria. Her departure from the Wartburg removed what must have been a nearly lifelong source of mortification to Elizabeth. But 1226 was a year to go down in history as one of floods, famine, and widespread plague. That plague, known in the Middle Ages as the pest, is called in our day smallpox, and it has been nearly wiped out by modern science. In the Middle Ages, however, people died by the thousands when the pest swept through the towns and cities.

An ancient historical chronicle says of the famine of 1226 that, because of men's sins, God afflicted the people in various ways—by the danger of sudden death and by a horrible epidemic of pestilence. Certainly for a long time the people lived in poverty, sickness, and more than ordinary misery.

As had happened so often before, Louis was away from home. Elizabeth, only nineteen years old, was in charge of the castle, the farms, and the villagers, as well as of the vassals in the many surrounding castles. To administer all that property and rule all those people in such a time of crisis would test the powers of an experienced ruler, but Elizabeth did not flinch from the task. Though she missed Louis sorely, she regarded his absence as the will of God.

It was not the usual politics, or war, or supervision of his property that took Louis away at such a time. It was the emperor. For twelve years Louis had waited for the call, and now he hastened to answer. Emperor Frederick was his dearest and truest friend, and Louis had vowed to follow him even to the ends of the earth.

"Dear Louis, it grieves me that you must wear this heavy armor", said Elizabeth, touching the hard metal in which Louis must ride and fight.

"But without it, little Sister, I would be killed before the battle had well begun", said Louis.

Elizabeth shuddered. How many times had she lain awake wondering if his armor would really protect him! How many times had she helped him put on the heavy padded shirt and trousers and watched his squire pull on the coat of mail and the leg and arm sections! After that came the metal cap and over that a fur one and last of all the helmet. Then Elizabeth could not see Louis at all. He was an iron man.

When the scarlet mantle with its golden lions had been slipped over his armor, Elizabeth was ready again for her part.

"Now let me fasten the crest on your helmet, Louis," she said as she attached the waving plumes, "and here is my scarlet kerchief for your favor."

"Thank you, little Sister", said Louis. "It will fly out over my head and protect me—but pray for me, too, Elizabeth. Your prayers always keep me safe."

"God bless you, dear Brother, and always watch over you!"

And Elizabeth turned back to her tremendous task of feeding the poor, caring for the sick, and managing the stores of grain and other goods so that everyone would receive a just share.

Louis did not like to leave her, but he believed that his duty to his emperor came first. Frederick had called a great council to be held in Cremona in Italy. Among the important affairs to be discussed was the coming crusade, for which Louis was waiting impatiently. Frederick's plans did not turn out well, however, and they were obliged to make a dangerous journey through northern Italy without accomplishing much of what he had hoped to do.

Emperor Frederick had not changed very much. He was still as courageous, charming, and confident as ever. He always traveled with a luxurious court. Hundreds of knights, squires, and servants kept his tent as comfortable, if not as safe, as his royal palace. He was constantly at war with enemies or with his own vassals, and at this particular time he was engaged in a bitter quarrel with the Pope. In spite of these things, Louis rode loyally and happily beside him. Like all medieval knights, both were willing to die for Christ and his Church, but they thought nothing of quarreling with the Pope.

But while Louis rode with the emperor in Italy, things went from bad to worse at the Wartburg Castle. As soon as the people began to realize that their small stores of grain were getting dangerously low, they stormed up the steep path to the castle. They demanded to see the landgravine, but the stewards barred the way. They knew well what their mistress would do, and they were responsible for keeping sufficient supplies in the castle for those who lived there. When Elizabeth heard about their actions, she wept and went down to the village with all the food she could find in the kitchens.

The winter was very cold, and life in a medieval castle, in spite of its grandeur, was never comfortable. Now, in this year of famine, fuel became a problem, too. Elizabeth's two little children were often cold, though she never let them go hungry. Little Hermann was four years old now and followed his mother wherever she went, begging her to tell him stories or sing gypsy songs. Sophie was just beginning to walk, but Guda or Isentrude usually carried her, since her legs were too short to climb the tall steps.

"Oh, look, Mother!" cried Hermann, gazing out at the snow-covered courtyard. "Everything's covered with sugar!"

Elizabeth explained about snow, but Hermann was still a little confused. When Guda offered him some sugar, he thanked her politely but said that he would rather not eat cold snow. Elizabeth laughed at that.

"I wonder if it will be as hard for us to get used to the ways of heaven as it is to learn about things on earth", she said. "If it is, we shall surely need a mother up there to help us!"

During much of the winter, Master Conrad was away on a preaching tour along the Rhine. Louis was gone. His brothers were also far away, riding with the emperor's troops. There was no one to advise Elizabeth or to help her make decisions. She was nearly twenty years old now, but that is not a great age for such responsibility. The stewards and other high officers, while they did not dare to disobey her outright, were determined not to let her give away the grain stored in the great cellar bins.

"How can I get grain for the poor, Guda?" asked Elizabeth anxiously. "I can't get the keys from the marshal, and I can't move those heavy bars."

"Both of us together could not move the bars", said Guda. "Perhaps God does not want you to touch those bins."

"Well, I know one thing that I can do. I still have all my beautiful Hungarian jewels. They will be good for something at last if I can sell them and get food for the poor.

"Surely you will not sell those!" said Guda. "They are part of your dowry. What will the landgrave say?"

"He will say that I did well. Come, Guda, we can get money, and the poor people can buy grain and milk for their children."

But soon the money that the jewels brought was gone. Elizabeth and her companions sold everything else that would bring in money. They went down to the village and comforted the poor and sick. Elizabeth even tried to milk a cow for one worried old peasant, but she was not very good at it. The cow kicked over the pail, and Elizabeth cried.

"Oh, I am good for nothing—for nothing at all!" She wept helplessly.

When all the money was gone, as well as most of the household expense money, Elizabeth ordered the stewards to open the granaries. They refused. They said that everyone in the castle would starve.

"We shall not starve", said Elizabeth. "God will not permit us to starve if we are generous. We must have faith."

All the knights and ladies of the castle, the stewards, the bailiffs, and the marshal stood in front of the granaries. The ladies screamed and sobbed. Some of the men cursed.

Elizabeth prayed and asked the angels to open the doors for her. The angels must have heard her, for the bailiffs gave up and opened the doors. Then Elizabeth became a baker. Every day more than nine hundred loaves were baked in the great ovens, and the hungry came to the castle for bread.

At last the cruel winter passed, and the worst seemed over, but suddenly the pest broke out in Eisenach. People died like flies in the streets. The bodies of the dead lay where they fell because no one would touch them.

Elizabeth took her children into the little chapel that Louis had made for her near her room. They all knelt before the altar.

"Lord God", prayed Elizabeth, "I commit to thee myself and my children and my whole household. Watch over me while I go to do thy will, and give me strength to do it."

Elizabeth nursed the sick and buried the dead. She made shrouds out of beautiful veils she had worn. The people took courage from her and began to help each other. But there were too many sick to be cared for, so Elizabeth built a small hospital at the foot of the road to the Wartburg. It was the first hospital in Germany to be built and run by lay people instead of by religious orders.

The summer was hot, and the odor of the sickness in the little hospital was unbearable. Guda and Isentrude were worn out. Elizabeth had to train nurses to help them. She taught the sick how to offer their pain and fear to God for their own souls and for the faithful departed. She never stopped her works of mercy until the plague was over.

The autumn came, and the crops were good. The people looked up again and were glad. Then came terrible rains. Would the harvest be lost again?

"If there were only one just spirit among us to whom God would listen", said Elizabeth, "he would spare the people."

She never dreamed that she herself was that chosen soul and that because of her God ended the floods, spared the crops, and sent his angel to drive the plague out of Eisenach. When miracles occurred, it was always to her the goodness of God alone. She thought they happened in spite of her unworthiness!

So the terrible time came slowly to an end, and, best of all, Louis came home. Elizabeth had someone to confide in now. The money was gone, and the grain must be nearly gone, but Louis would understand.

The bailiffs accused Elizabeth of giving everything away and leaving the castle in poverty.

"Let her give to the poor what she likes", said Louis. "If the castle still stands, I am content."

They took him down to the granaries to show him how little grain was left. As they came near, the golden grain ran out under the door. The bins were so full that the grain was running over. Louis turned to Elizabeth.

"How have the poor people fared during this cruel winter?"

And Elizabeth answered, "I have given God what is God's, and he has preserved for us what is yours and mine."

9

"GOOD-BYE, DEAR BROTHER"

IT WAS A WARM DAY in early spring. Elizabeth and
Louis were sitting in the sunshine out on the ter-
race, enjoying each other's company after his long
absence.

"But you are so thin and pale, little Sister! Does
Master Conrad let you have enough to eat?"

Elizabeth laughed.

"That is like a puzzle with no answer," she said, "but I can always have bread made out of wheat grown on our own farm, and I can soak it in some of your good wine. It is lucky that you planted all those vineyards."

"And the children? How do they fare? Little Hermann is straight and tall for his age. Each time I come home, he is taller."

"Sophie is the practical one. She is just like your mother. Perhaps that is because she is named for her. As for Hermann . . ."

Elizabeth told Louis about Hermann and the snow sugar.

"That boy has imagination", said Louis. "He may become a poet like some of the great ones who used to sing in the Festival Hall when my father was alive."

Louis had his pouch in his hand. He tossed it across to Elizabeth.

"There's a little present in there for you", he said. "See if you can find it."

Elizabeth eagerly opened the pouch and began to search through the contents. Suddenly her face turned white. She was clutching a bit of black cloth that made her heart almost stop beating. It was one of the small black crosses that the bishops gave to those who were about to start on a crusade. Louis had taken the cross!

"Oh, Louis, dear Louis—"

Elizabeth fell into Louis' arms, almost fainting. He held her close and tried to comfort her. He had forgotten that the cross was in his pouch.

"Dear little Sister, I did not tell you before because I did not want you to be thinking about it so long."

"Oh, Louis, I *want* you to go! I *do* want you to go—but I *don't* want you to go. Do you understand?"

"Yes, I understand. I understand very well. I don't want to leave you and the children, either, but I must defend the holy places for the love of Christ. It has always been the custom for the landgraves of Thuringia to take the cross. One of my ancestors died with Frederick Barbarossa. He was called Louis the Pious, and I was named for him. Don't you remember how you wanted to be a crusader yourself when you were little?"

Elizabeth nodded. Big tears rolled down her cheeks. She covered her face with her hands and wept silently for a minute or two. She thought that her heart would break. Then she lifted her head and stood up. She folded Louis' hands and folded her own over them.

"Dear Louis, I will not hold you back. It is the will of God. I have given myself entirely to him, and now I must give you, too. May he give us strength to obey him!"

It was high time for Emperor Frederick to start his crusade. When he had been proclaimed emperor more than eleven years earlier, he had promised Pope Innocent III to organize a crusade as soon as possible. But Frederick was always kept busy with worldly matters. He kept putting it off.

Pope Innocent died, and Pope Honorius succeeded

him. He crowned the emperor in Rome, and Frederick promised a German army for the crusade—but he was not ready yet. When Gregory IX became Pope, he accepted no promises. He gave orders—and Frederick had to go. So it was that now in 1227 he was actually assembling his troops, and Landgrave Louis of Thuringia was at home in his Wartburg Castle making all the complicated arrangements necessary for a ruler who was going on a journey from which he might not return.

One of the first things that he did was to have a Passion play performed at the church in Eisenach. Miracle plays were well known to the people. They had often been performed both in the churches and the castles. Usually they were about the birth of Christ or the Resurrection. A play based on the sufferings and death of our Lord was something new. All the parts were played by priests and students from religious schools, and the mournful "Lament for Our Lady" moved everyone to tears. It may well have been the *Stabat Mater*, which is still used in the Lenten liturgy.

Louis thought that the play would be a fitting beginning for the crusade, and he invited knights and ladies from all the neighboring castles. The play was performed on a big wooden stage built in front of the church. Servants and villagers sat in the audience right beside the nobility. For every knight who went to battle there were dozens of horsemen, foot soldiers, drummers, trumpeters, gong-bearers, armorers, cooks, hostlers, wagon drivers, barbers, and other servants. They were as much a part of the crusade as the knights whom they served. Their wives and families loved them just as much and grieved just as much at their departure. Fine ladies and lowly peasants wept together at the Passion play and sympathized with each other.

Soon afterward, Louis journeyed to the Kreuzburg Castle, where his son Hermann had been born. There he called together all those knights, vassals, and other nobles who were to remain at home. He made a speech to them, urging them to take good care of the women and children and to administer all his property loyally and honorably.

"Our country is at peace", said Louis. "Everywhere you look, you can see undisturbed peace. Now I am leaving my peaceful kingdom. I am leaving my beloved wife, my little children, and all that I hold dear, and I am going forth as a pilgrim in the name of Jesus Christ. I beg of you all to pray for me daily, that if it be the will of God I may return safe and sound to my family and my kingdom."

There were no women in the audience, only knights who had followed Louis into battle or had known him as a just and generous sovereign. But there were tears in the eyes of all who heard him, for Louis was greatly loved by his people.

What about Elizabeth? What arrangements were to be made for her? She was expecting her third child within a few months, and Louis knew that he would not be at home when the baby arrived. He wanted to talk to Elizabeth about the future, so he asked Walter of Varila to saddle their horses. Then the beloved Landgrave Louis and his gentle young wife, the Landgravine Elizabeth, rode off through the countryside in the spring sunshine and talked of things to come. They did not gallop as in the earlier days. They walked their horses quietly and talked.

"Elizabeth, you know that this is a dangerous journey I am undertaking and that I may not come back."

"I know, dear Brother", answered Elizabeth in a small whisper.

"Will it satisfy you if I appoint my brother Henry as regent for little Hermann in case of necessity?"

"Yes, Louis—anything you say."

"Then there is the child that is to come. Shall we dedicate that child to God?"

"Yes, Louis. We are all in the hands of God now. He will take care of the little one, too."

Louis was silent for a while, and Elizabeth could think of nothing to say. Then Louis spoke again.

"Elizabeth, if the new child is a boy, let us entrust his education to the Benedictine monks. But if it is a girl, let her be sent to the Premonstratensian Convent and be trained with the nuns."

"It shall be done as you will, dear Brother. Shall we visit the Benedictines today?"

The two were so sad at leaving each other that they found it hard to talk at all. They rode all that day and again the next, visiting every convent, abbey, and monastery within riding distance. Everywhere Louis asked for prayers and knelt for a blessing, and everywhere the monks and nuns whom both Louis and Elizabeth had befriended promised that they would pray for him constantly.

There were still many plans to be made. Master Conrad, who had returned to the castle from a preaching tour, seems to have been a little more gentle, seeing the courage and resignation with which Elizabeth met this hard trial. Louis respected Conrad's honesty and good judgment in religious matters, and he placed in his charge the direction of the many churches, monasteries, and convents built by the landgrave and his family.

Landgravine Sophie had come up from Eisenach as soon as she had heard the news. To her Louis commended his little family, and to his brothers he entrusted the business affairs of the kingdom. For Henry there was one especially important message.

"Do you remember, Henry, that our father asked us to destroy the castle at Eitersburg because it was a source of harm to a nearby monastery?"

"Yes," said Henry. "I remember."

"You know, too, that our father's will has not been done. If I should die on this crusade, I want you to promise me, Henry, to destroy that castle at once. Burn it to the ground."

"I promise", said Henry. "It shall be done."

The time was now growing short. Crusaders from the whole countryside were gathering at the Thuringian border. Louis must go at last.

Elizabeth wondered at herself. "How many times", she said to Guda, "have I seen him raise his lance in salute and heard him call out, 'For God and my lady!' How many, many times—but it was never like this, Guda."

"He will come back, my lady", said Guda, with a confidence she did not feel. "The landgrave is strong and brave. He is the greatest leader of them all. Never fear. He will come back."

Elizabeth shook her head. "It is the will of God", she said.

The noise and confusion of a medieval army getting under way was tremendous. The clanking of armor, the shouts of the mule drivers and wagoners, the din of trumpets and drums, and the rattle of heavy wheels on cobblestones drowned out the last farewells of the families and friends.

Elizabeth had begged to be allowed to ride with Louis part of the way, and, as usual, he could not refuse her. When the last moment arrived, she was beside him, mounted and ready to start. Everyone was gathered at the gate to see him off. No one felt like talking. People stood in silence. Louis kissed his mother and asked for her blessing. Then he kissed the children and other members of his family and made the Sign of the Cross over each one.

It was the eve of the feast of Saint John the Baptist. On that June evening every year, great bonfires were lighted on hills and high places. All over the country-side the flames rose in tall columns and flickered as if they answered each other from one hilltop to another. In the villages there was singing and dancing, but when the merrymakers saw the long line of crusaders riding by, they stopped to ask Saint John to protect those brave servants of God.

Late that night the cavalcade stopped for a few hours of rest. The next day Elizabeth looked sick with weariness, but she would not turn back.

"When we come to the Thuringian border, please go back, Elizabeth. All the armies will meet there, and I must command the German troops."

All too soon they reached the border and stopped for their last farewell. They dismounted and stood beside their horses. The knights who were with them waited at some distance. Louis reached into his pouch—the same pouch in which Elizabeth had found the black cross—and took out a ring.

"Dear Sister, dear little Sister," he said, "look carefully at this ring."

Elizabeth had seen it many times. It was set with a large sapphire, on which was engraved an *Agnus Dei*. Louis used it as a seal when he signed state documents.

"If anyone ever brings this ring to you, you must believe the message of the bearer. He may come with a message from me alive, or with the news of my death. Whatever it is, it will be true."

Elizabeth put her hand on the ring, and Louis put his hand on hers.

"May God in heaven protect you, little Sister. With his help you will be able to carry out what we have agreed upon."

So they parted. Elizabeth rode back to the castle and dressed herself in common black clothes, like a village widow. She filled her days with prayer and penance, with care of the sick and poor, and she waited for her child.

While Elizabeth lived out her dreary days, Louis rode on to meet his emperor. The journey was long and hard—through Germany, over the Alps into Italy, down, down through Lombardy and Tuscany to Brindisi. There the two friends met, on the feast of Saint Stephen, and rode on happily together, picking up reinforcements as they went and making great plans for the attack on Jerusalem.

"I have promised to bring Elizabeth a little earth from Bethlehem, where our Lord was born", said Louis.

"And you must not forget a vial of water from the River Jordan", replied Frederick. "It is said to have great healing power."

When they came to the port of Brindisi, where they were to set sail, the heat was overpowering. Camping conditions were very bad. The soldiers were dissatisfied. Some of the rulers would not permit their troops to stay. There was a great deal of fever among the men, and many died. Soon Louis, usually so strong and healthy, began to feel sick, but he was unwilling to admit it.

The emperor himself suffered much from the terrible heat and was advised to rest, but he wanted to go on. Louis could hardly hold up his head, but he followed. They went to a small island named Sant' Andrea, near the entrance of the port, each traveling in his own ship with his own knights. There it was evident that Louis had a high fever, but they sailed on to Otranto in spite of it. Then Louis could go no farther.

"My lord emperor," he said, "my time has come. I am sick unto death. Send quickly for a priest so that I may receive the last rites."

The patriarch of Jerusalem and another bishop came at once. Louis' personal chaplain, Berthold, who always traveled with him, stayed by his side, and the dying landgrave received the last sacraments with great devotion.

Berthold was watching his master anxiously. Louis lay with closed eyes. Suddenly, he opened them and looked at Berthold.

"Do you see all those white doves? When they go, I am going, too."

Those were the last words spoken by the noble Landgrave Louis of Thuringia, a brave and gentle knight who died in the service of God at the age of twenty-seven, in the year 1227. The doves flew off toward the east, and the soul of Louis followed.

The body of Elizabeth's beloved Louis was wrapped in linen dipped in wax, and a solemn Mass was sung in Otranto for his soul. He would have been sorely grieved to know that the emperor had to give up the crusade because of the plague. Surely he must have looked down from his heavenly home with pride and affection when Frederick, some time later, actually did carry out the crusade and was crowned king of Jerusalem.

Back in the Wartburg Castle, meanwhile, Elizabeth followed in her mind the journey that Louis had undertaken, trying to imagine where he was and what he was doing, and praying for him constantly.

On September 29, about three weeks after the death of Louis, Elizabeth's third child was born— a girl. Elizabeth named her Gertrude, after her own mother.

At the very same time, the terrible news of the landgrave's death reached the village. The weary messengers took their sad message to Henry and Conrad, Louis' brothers, who sought out their mother at the convent and told her. Who would tell Elizabeth?

In her own room, holding her little daughter in her arms, lay the Landgravine Elizabeth. Louis' mother and some of the court ladies came to the door, and the young mother held up the baby to show them.

"See! She is the image of her father. Dear Louis! How happy he will be!"

But Landgravine Sophie did not smile. The ladies were silent. Elizabeth stared at them, frightened.

"My dear daughter," said Sophie, "do not mourn too much at the fate that God has meted out to your husband, who is also my very dear son."

Elizabeth thought that Louis had been taken prisoner.

"But we can free him", she began. "Let us begin . . ."

"Dear daughter," said Sophie, "he is dead."

She handed to Elizabeth the sapphire ring with the Lamb of God engraved on it. Elizabeth was stunned. At first she could not believe it. Then she became delirious with grief. She left the baby and ran from room to room, crying out in despair, "Dead! Dead! Dead! Oh, not this! Not this!"

At last, in her aimless running, she struck her head violently against a wall and fell to the ground.

Guda and Isentrude finally got her back to her room where she threw herself on the floor and wept bitterly. This was the only time that any of her mother's violence appeared in Elizabeth. God had taken from her the one thing on earth to which she had clung with all her heart. It was for her the end of life.

"My dear Brother is dead", moaned Elizabeth. "Now shall the world and all its joys be dead to me, too."

10

HARDNESS SOFTENED BY
THE OIL OF JOY

"ELIZABETH!"

The voice was a roar. A heavy fist pounded the table until the glass goblets jumped. The voice and the fist belonged to Henry, brother of Louis, guardian of little Hermann, and now lord of the Wartburg.

"Eat what you find on the table whether you know where it comes from or not. You have embarrassed us long enough by your whims."

It was the third hard winter in village and castle. The weather was bitter cold, food was scarce, and tempers were short in the Wartburg. Henry and Conrad meant well, but they did not understand Elizabeth. Without Louis to protect her, she was treated with little respect. Henry scolded and Conrad sneered. To them she was merely odd and unreasonable. She made everybody uncomfortable, they said. Nobody likes to have his conscience prodding him constantly, and that was the effect that Elizabeth seemed to have on other people.

Landgravine Sophie stayed at the castle and tried to defend Elizabeth. There was now a strong bond between them. They had both loved Louis deeply. But, in spite of Sophie's sympathy, Elizabeth was ill-treated in the castle. It is hard to say whether Henry and Conrad deliberately turned people against her, but they certainly did nothing to protect her. Guda and Isentrude shuddered at the cruel talk they heard again, just as in the olden days when Elizabeth was the little strange princess from Hungary. Even then she had disturbed all the ladies of the court by being "too pious", "too religious", or by "trying to act holy".

Down in the village the people whispered what they had heard from servants in the castle.

"She wasted all the landgrave's money—gave it to undeserving beggars."

"Yes, and remember how she gave away the precious grain right and left? She should never have been trusted with money."

"It is a good thing that Prince Henry knows how to be firm with her. He has put strong locks on the granaries and gives her no money at all. Louis was always too lenient."

The minds of the people were poisoned against Elizabeth. The very ones whom she had nursed and cared for turned against her now.

One dark, cold night she suddenly made up her mind. She walked down the icy path to the village, leaning on a cane for safety's sake. She planned to find some place for herself and the children to live. There were lights in several houses, and she tried one door after another.

"Who is there?"

"The landgravine. May I come in?"

Silence. No one would open. At last a tavernkeeper took pity on her and let her stay in an old tool shed.

"I will drive out the pigs, my lady," he said, "so that you can sleep."

Some old work clothes hung on a hook. These he put on a bench and over her knees and left her. There she sat in the cold until dawn. Then she heard the Mass bell from the Franciscan church.

The friars were chanting their morning prayers when they saw in the half darkness the figure of the landgravine. She walked toward the altar, surrounded by the light of their candles as by a glory, and began in a clear voice to sing the *Te Deum*. After a startled moment, the friars joined her. She was welcome in the house of God.

Elizabeth had always wanted to give up everything and be a beggar like Brother Francis. This was her chance. Guda and Isentrude brought the children down to her, and she took them with her as she begged from house to house. But door after door was shut in her face. The royal princess, Elizabeth of Hungary, Landgravine of Thuringia, accompanied by the royal children, was turned away by her subjects. Guda and Isentrude wept bitterly.

A poor priest gave them shelter and a bed of straw, but orders came from the castle that they must all move immediately to the home of a certain nobleman who was an especial enemy of Elizabeth. Unwilling to offend Henry, he did give them a small, dark room, but refused food, heat, or any other comfort. The next day Elizabeth took her little family back to the friendly tavernkeeper's shed. Before she left, she touched the walls of the room as she used to do as a child in the Wartburg Castle.

"Thank you, kind walls," she said, "for sheltering us against the weather as well as you could. I should like to thank your master, but I have nothing to thank him for."

Of course Elizabeth could not keep the children with her in the kind of life she was leading. She had to send them to trusted friends of their father—at least for a time. She herself continued to live in the shed, supporting herself by spinning and weaving. Something deep in her heart had made her turn from the medieval idea of servant and master. Long, long before the rest of the world would accept the doctrine of brotherhood, she, like Brother Francis, believed in the equality of man. She preferred poverty to luxury made possible by the misery and labor of serfs and slaves. In spite of her sufferings, she was happy to be like Christ.

Now came a new turn of events. Elizabeth had an aunt and an uncle, sister and brother of her mother, Queen Gertrude. Her aunt was the abbess of a convent, and her uncle, lord bishop of Bamberg. They heard of Elizabeth's troubles through Landgravine Sophie, and the abbess immediately sent carriages to bring Elizabeth and the children to her convent.

"Mother! Mother!" The children caught her around the waist and pulled her face down to kiss her.

"Don't leave us again, Mother. Stay with us all the time", said Hermann soberly. He was old enough to understand some of the things he heard.

"Take *me*, Mother, take *me!*" begged little Sophie when she saw her mother reach for baby Gertrude in Guda's arms.

"My little ones! My little ones!" There were tears in Elizabeth's eyes as she tried to hold them all at once. Now her heart was torn again. Something of the world always caught at the hem of her garment, even as she reached toward heaven.

While they stayed at the convent, Elizabeth gratefully followed the daily routine of the nuns. Guda and Isentrude were relieved and happy, and the children became the pets of all the nuns. As soon as possible, the bishop of Bamberg gave Elizabeth a castle that he considered a suitable place for a princess to live, and he himself paid the expenses of running it.

One day the lord bishop's carriage drove up to the gate of the castle. Elizabeth ran down to meet him, and he was struck by the fact that, in spite of all her fastings, sufferings, and lack of sleep, she was still very beautiful. Even in her black widow's gown, she looked every inch a queen. That pleased him, because he had come on a special mission.

"Elizabeth," said the lord bishop, "I come with an important message. You know that the Empress Isabelle has died. I now have the honor to tell you that our great emperor, Frederick, wishes you to become his wife."

"The emperor!"

"Yes, Elizabeth, and if you accept his offer the whole world will be at your feet."

Elizabeth was bewildered. She remembered how Satan had once taken Christ up into a high place and offered him all the world and its glory. She shut her eyes, for this was a great temptation. To be the empress, ruler over the entire Christian world!

What an example she could set of what a Christian ruler should be! Perhaps this was what God wanted her to do. But she had loved Louis so much! No, she could not marry another. She said so to the lord bishop, but he would not take that as a final answer.

"Take time to make your decision", said the lord bishop. "This is a very great honor, and I urge you most strongly to accept it."

Whenever Elizabeth's soul was troubled, she sought the help of God. All her possessions had been taken away from her. She was persecuted. She did not know how to protect her own children. Now she was tormented by a temptation. What should she do? What was it right for her to do?

"We are going on a pilgrimage", said Elizabeth to Guda and Isentrude. "We are going to Bavaria, where my mother was born."

The three companions set out for a village in Bavaria where one of her uncles had built a monastery. They found lodgings in the village and then climbed a wooded slope to the monastery, where there was a famous shrine to the Blessed Virgin. Before they left the village, Elizabeth took something white from her baggage. She carried it up the hill and laid it at the feet of our Lady. It was her wedding gown-the beautiful white damask in which she had danced so happily on her wedding night.

Elizabeth had made her decision. Once, long ago, when she was a little girl, she had laid her golden coronet at the feet of her thorn-crowned Savior. Now she laid the crown of an empress at the feet of His most holy Mother.

Far away in Rome, Pope Gregory IX had heard of Elizabeth. He had learned of all the troubles that had beset her since the death of her husband, and he wished to assure her of his protection. To Master Conrad, who had returned from another long preaching tour, he gave orders to see to it that Elizabeth's personal possessions were restored to her and that she received her proper inheritance as widow of the landgrave. Master Conrad was also told to arrange for the legal rights of the children.

The Pope knew of Elizabeth's search for sanctity. He had heard about her fasts and vigils and her boundless charity. Now he wrote a letter to encourage and comfort her:

"From the small seed of tears you may gain endless furrows of happiness in all eternity."

The Pope knew well that those who sow in sorrow reap in joy. Like Master Conrad, he believed that Elizabeth was on the road to sainthood, and he had no intention of interfering with her progress by softness or sympathy.

"May all that you suffer be hard and cruel", said Pope Gregory. "But the hardness shall be softened by the oil of joy. All crooked things shall be made straight and all roughnesses made smooth."

While these things were happening to Elizabeth, a sad procession was moving slowly upward through Italy and across the mountains into Germany. A company of knights who had been close friends of Louis and had set out with him for Jerusalem were bringing the body of their beloved landgrave back to his home in Thuringia.

On the back of a mule was placed the black coffin in which the whitened bones of the landgrave rested. On top lay a silver crucifix set with many precious stones. This was a symbol that a crusader lay in the casket. The knights traveled by day and rested at night at the nearest church or monastery. In every place they stopped, the people gathered reverently and watched beside the coffin all the night with lighted candles. In the morning, Mass was said for the crusader's soul, and wherever the procession stopped the knights left as a gift the embroidered cloth that had covered the coffin.

As the procession neared the city of Bamberg, where Elizabeth was living, a rider hurried ahead to tell the bishop, who immediately sent a message to Elizabeth:

"Go at once to meet the body of your dear husband and lord."

Now was Elizabeth's cup of sorrow full to the brim. She longed to hide somewhere and cry her heart out, but she was still the landgravine. She must go to meet all that was left of her husband, the beloved Louis of Thuringia. Guda and Isentrude stayed close to their mistress, as always, and all three set out to join the people gathering in the church square as their kind-hearted bishop had asked them to do.

Slowly, mournfully, tolled the great bell. The bishop had gone on ahead with a company of priests and monks, school pupils, and laymen of the city, carrying candles and chanting the *De Profundis*. People from nearby villages had joined them, and by the time the weary Thuringian bearers had placed before the altar the coffin bearing the mortal remains of their master, the church was full.

The coffin was opened, and Elizabeth gazed, dry-eyed, at the little heap of white bones that had been her strong, kind, loving Louis. Then she turned and walked with queenly dignity to the square in front of the church. There she seated herself on a stone bench and called before her the faithful knights who had brought him back to his own country. After she had spoken her grateful thanks, she told them of all that had happened to her since the death of Louis. The knights were shocked and angry.

"My lady," said one, "we lay our swords at your feet."

"We pledge ourselves to defend you, my lady," said another, "and to restore your possessions to you."

"You and your children must return at once to the Wartburg Castle", said still another, "and rule the kingdom as our noble landgrave would have wished you to do."

Good, faithful Walter of Varila had come to help Elizabeth and to return with the body of Louis. He was at her side now. So were Guda and Isentrude. They never left her until the funeral procession reached the monastery of Reinhardtsbrunn, where Louis was laid to rest at last after the long, weary journey.

As soon as the monks had laid the landgrave in his grave, two groups gathered outside the monastery. The people watched with interest.

"See, there is Landgravine Sophie with her sons. Henry looks black with anger."

"But look at Landgravine Elizabeth! All the landgrave's knights are with her. There will be a quarrel."

"Ssh! Here comes Walter of Varila. He is a brave and courteous knight. He is going to talk to Henry. Listen!"

Walter of Varila spoke so that all could hear.

"We, the knights of Landgrave Louis of the Wartburg Castle, are grieved and shamed at the rumors we have heard. Here is his widow, the Princess Elizabeth, daughter of the king of Hungary, whom you were bound to respect and honor and whom you should have consoled in her grief. Instead, you have turned her out to beg for a living. Her children, heirs to the throne of Thuringia, are being cared for by strangers. This is a disgrace to Thuringia and a dishonor to the name of our beloved landgrave, who gave his life in the service of God. If you do not restore to this good and saintly woman her rights and privileges as land-gravine, it is our solemn belief that the wrath of God will fall heavily upon us all and upon the kingdom of Thuringia."

There was a hushed silence when Varila stopped speaking. Everyone looked at Henry, who had not taken his eyes from Varila's face. God must have touched his heart at that moment, for suddenly he broke down and sobbed.

"You are right, Varila. You are right. I have not treated Elizabeth as Louis would have had me do. I am ashamed and sorry, and I will do all I can to regain her friendship and restore her rights."

Landgravine Sophie, standing with troubled eyes behind her sons, reached out and touched Henry's shoulder with pride and relief. These three young people facing each other were the children she had brought up. They had played together, and they had all loved Louis. Even now they were only in their early twenties. Elizabeth was twenty-two, and Henry only a year older. Conrad was even younger. They still made errors of judgment.

Thank God!" she thought. "Now I can go back to the convent and live out my days in peace."

Henry went over to Elizabeth and was about to kneel before her, but she refused to let him do so. Instead, she thanked him for his kindness and forgave him from her heart. It seemed as if everything would now go well and that Elizabeth could order her life as she wished. But it was not to be so. Not everyone agreed with Henry about bringing her back to the castle. Things had been much livelier and more comfortable without her. Those who enjoyed rich food could eat to their hearts' content, and those who didn't want to get up in time for Mass could stay in bed. Guda and Isentrude were not surprised to hear the same old complaints.

Master Conrad returned to the Wartburg for a while, and his presence protected Elizabeth. Soon, however, he had to go back to Marburg to start a new tour of preaching. Elizabeth turned to Henry, who had kept the promise he made to Varila. She told Henry about the Pope's letter.

"May all that you suffer be hard and cruel", the Pope had said.

"But, Elizabeth, you have already suffered so much", said Henry. "It is better to stay here where you belong and bring your children up in peace."

Henry was kind, but Elizabeth felt that she could never, in the life of the Wartburg Castle, reach the holiness for which her soul longed. When Henry failed to persuade her to stay, he offered her the city of Marburg, which was in Hesse, a state ruled by the Thuringian landgraves. He would also give her a suitable income and some property, as well as anything remaining of what she had brought from Hungary. There wasn't much left. Even the silver cradle had been sold during the famine.

Elizabeth accepted Henry's offer. Arrangements were made about the children and their rights, and necessary papers signed. For the present she would take the children with her. She was free at last.

Down the steep path from the Wartburg Castle she went for the last time. With her went Guda and Isentrude, and one cannot help thinking, remembering the patience, the fortitude, and the loyalty of those two faithful companions, that they were not far from being saints themselves.

11

A WISH FULFILLED AT LAST

"AND WHAT DO YOU THINK of our landgravine now?" asked one stout burgher's wife of another.

"The same as I did before", returned the other. "I think she is out of her mind."

"Have you seen the place where she lives?"

"I have—and it isn't suitable for a woodcutter's shelter."

"Oh, but you should have seen the hut that she lived in when she first came. It was hardly fit for pigs to live in. This one is at least made of sturdy wood and clay. But it is still a disgrace to Marburg."

"Well, of course, there's the hospital. That is large and comfortable and has a fine garden. It must be admitted that the Landgravine Elizabeth is generous with everyone but herself."

The first speaker shifted her heavy basket.

"I hear that the fine ladies of the city are very much disappointed. They expected dances, hunts, and tournaments, but the castle remains dark. I wonder what the lord bishop thinks of his niece."

"He is probably much disturbed. He has done all he can to make her live as a lady should."

"To tell the truth, I don't know what to think of her. I hear that some ladies have gone to that little hut of hers and that she has given them excellent advice. In the hospital they call her a saint."

The burgher's wife shifted her basket again.

"Well, we shall see what we shall see." The two nodded at each other and went about their business.

Elizabeth did not know it, but she was now beginning the steepest and hardest part of her journey toward sanctity. Far up ahead shone the glory of God, and Elizabeth fixed her eyes upon it. She wanted to do nothing, to have nothing, to be nothing but what God wanted—but she still was not quite sure.

The pleasures of the world had always attracted

Elizabeth powerfully. She loved to dance and sing and receive compliments. It had cost her a great deal every time she gave up any of these things. Court gossips had hurt her more than she ever let anyone know except Guda and Isentrude. She had asked God to take away from her these desires and weaknesses, and now he seemed to be answering her.

"Let me renounce everything. Let me become just a beggar for Christ", she pleaded.

"No!" thundered Master Conrad. "Give up your will. Keep your possessions and use them for the poor. Join an order of nuns. This hermit's life is not proper for you."

But Elizabeth had one wish left, one thing she felt sure would help her soul to find peace. That was to join the Third Order founded by Brother Francis for married persons and others who wanted to serve God in a special way and yet remain free to attend to worldly duties. She could renew the vows of obedience, poverty, and chastity she had taken after her husband's death and dedicate the remainder of her life to the service of God in the world.

"If I am to climb, I must have steps under my feet", said Elizabeth.

So Master Conrad agreed. Since he was so frequently absent, Elizabeth would at least have some order and direction and a fixed rule of life. Elizabeth chose Good Friday as the day to make her vows. Then all the altars would be stripped, as she hoped to strip her soul of earthly affections. She placed her hands upon the altar in the Franciscan church and renounced everything, even her children, for the love of God. Her hair was cut and the gray Franciscan habit slipped over her head and tied with a white cord. She was the first woman to take the veil in the Third Order. As always, Guda and Isentrude followed her.

But what of the children? They had been perfectly happy in the bare little house with their mother to sing to them and play with them. Hermann, though, must soon become a page and be trained for the life of the castle. Elizabeth prayed God to take away her earthly love for her children. She wanted to have the courage of Abraham when he was ready to slay his only son at God's word. And God heard her. Suddenly she was able to think of them only as the children of Louis and to surrender them willingly to his family. Hermann and Sophie were sent back to the Kreuzburg Castle, and two-year-old Gertrude was sent to the Premonstratensian Convent as Louis and Elizabeth had agreed.

It might seem that hard decisions were easy for Elizabeth. They were not, for saints are not saints while they are on earth. They are poor, weak human beings, and every time they beat down their own wills and renounce that which is comfortable, or agreeable, or even necessary, it hurts them just as much as it would hurt anyone else. How could Elizabeth possibly get along with so little sleep, so little food, and still have strength to do what she did for the poor and carry on her duties in the castle? She did not even have daily Communion to sustain her. Only the grace of God can explain it. She prayed for that—and she paid for it.

The rule of the Third Order was much stricter than it is today. Those who belonged to it recited the canonical hours, wore habits of poor, cheap cloth, fasted from All Saints' Day until Easter, abstained four days a week, and renounced all worldly pleasures. Elizabeth found herself completely at home in the order. She had long been following a much stricter rule herself.

One thing that displeased Master Conrad was Elizabeth's inability to manage money. If it came into her hands, she gave it away. He thought she was disobedient rather than impractical, and he punished her, but nothing could darken the light of her happiness. She had her hospital. She served the poor. Over and over again, as in earlier days, she saw the face of Christ in that of some beggar or sick person. She waited on all of them personally, especially the most loathsome cases, and her happy face lighted the hospital halls and the streets of Marburg.

Elizabeth was none too skillful at manual work. She had been brought up with many servants to wait on her. Her spinning was not very successful. The needle broke when she mended her patched garments, and she burned holes in the pan when she was cooking her tasteless, unsalted meals. She was supposed to be the doorkeeper at the hospital, but often when Master

Conrad arrived she was absent from her post. She might be carrying some moaning child back and forth in her arms and singing to him or washing the feet of some poor, dusty patient who had walked miles to the hospital.

Elizabeth's carelessness with money angered Master Conrad. He told her that she could give only one penny at a time. Of what use was a penny to anyone? Elizabeth had some silver pennies coined in the mint. She did give them away one at a time, but she let the beggars come back again and again until they had enough.

Then Master Conrad refused to let her handle money at all. She could distribute only bread. She gave away so many loaves that he said she could give only one slice at a time. Elizabeth could not offer a single slice of bread to a hungry beggar. Very well. She could give nothing at all. Elizabeth actually became sick with sorrow. She could not bear to see anyone suffering and not do anything about it.

One day there was a great commotion at the village inn.

"Did you see him? Did you see him? Such a handsome knight!"

"And what a charger he rides! Did you ever see such trappings? There must be a fortune in jewels on the saddlecloth alone."

"And the little golden bells on the bridle! There must be a hundred!"

"Who can he be, traveling with so many squires and servants? He does not speak our language."

Whoever he was, the richly clothed knight was in search of a Hungarian princess who was said to be living in Marburg as a hermitess. The bystanders were delighted to show him where Elizabeth lived as soon as they understood the few German words he knew.

The knight was Count Banfy of Hungary. It had been heard in that country that Elizabeth was in want, and King Andrew had sent the count to bring his daughter home. The count knelt before her and kissed her hand. There was no chair to offer him, so he sat on a wooden stool and tried to persuade Elizabeth to come home to her father's court. It was not seemly, he pointed out, for a Hungarian princess to be living in such poverty.

Elizabeth thanked the count with tears in her eyes for his kindness and for the long journey he had made, but she would not go.

"Thank you, thank you, Count Banfy, but tell my father that I am happier here than in any castle. Ask him to pray for me and to ask the court to do so. Tell my good father that I shall always pray for him."

Master Conrad, obeying the Pope's order, saw to it that Prince Henry sent regularly to Elizabeth the money that was due for her property. One day Henry sent her an unusually large sum. Master Conrad was away preaching. Elizabeth decided to give a great feast for the poor. They had so little joy on earth. Pennies or loaves of bread were not enough. They should have something happy to remember.

Elizabeth sent messengers with horns and trumpets for twelve miles in all directions to gather the crippled and sick into one great meadow near the city. They came—on foot, on mules, in hard wooden wagons, on the backs of neighbors. Some of the old tales say that there were as many as twelve thousand.

Everyone was to receive one gift, and all were to be fed and sheltered overnight if necessary. Loaves of bread were distributed, and each man, woman, and child received six pennies. Elizabeth walked among them like the empress she might have been, smiling, excited, childishly happy to be doing so much good at one time. As darkness fell, all of a sudden she had a wonderful idea.

"Fires! Let us light fires and make it look like a real festival!"

The fires were lighted, and the light of joy shone in the eyes of the poor. They began to sing, and Elizabeth sang with them. It was indeed a night to remember.

When Master Conrad returned, he was far from pleased. He was angry—and he was troubled, too. He never could understand that childlike quality in Elizabeth that made the festival with its blazing fires seem so reasonable. Perhaps he was afraid that in some way she would fail in her upward struggle and that he would be responsible.

Soon another strange knight appeared at the inn in Marburg. No handsome knight on a prancing charger this time—just kind, tired, old Walter of Varila coming to see if he could not persuade his little princess to go home. He did not really expect her to go. He had known her too long. But his promise to King Andrew lay heavily on his conscience. He had sworn to protect the princess, and he must keep his oath.

"How can you be so happy in such surroundings?" asked the good old knight.

"I am trying to reach the Kingdom of heaven, Varila. It is only a little way. All it needs is a little courage. Pray for me, Varila. I am happy because I have a hope of heaven, and I am trying to follow in the footsteps of Christ."

One day Master Conrad appeared at the door. His face was stern. Elizabeth rose. So did Guda and Isentrude. They were in fear at what he might say. He wasted no time.

"Search your soul, Elizabeth. Have you renounced everything?"

"Yes, Master Conrad."

"Then you must renounce these friends of yours. They must leave you at once!"

Now indeed Elizabeth was to be stripped of everything. Guda and Isentrude had been with her since she was four years old. They were almost a part of herself. For a long time they had been her only human consolation. Elizabeth's body shook. She felt faint.

"Have you the courage to stand alone with God?" thundered Master Conrad.

"Yes, Master Conrad."

Elizabeth bowed her head. She turned away and did not look at Guda and Isentrude as they prepared to go, sick at heart.

Master Conrad would not have Elizabeth live alone. He sent her a rough, ill-mannered young peasant girl and a very deaf elderly woman who had an unpleasant disposition. These two were ordered to watch Elizabeth and report what she did. They were also to see that she had plenty of occasions to exercise patience.

There was very little for these disagreeable people to report. Elizabeth continued to live as she had been doing. She slept on boards, she ate no meat or fish, she prayed long into the night. She nursed the sick, encouraging them, singing to them, making them laugh when she could, and she gave away all she possessed. In everything she followed Saint Francis and gave a worthy example for all time to his Third Order.

It was now the year of our Lord 1231. Elizabeth was twenty-four. In dark November of that year Master Conrad became very ill. He sent for Elizabeth. If he should die, who would direct her? What would become of this soul entrusted to him, this soul so far on the road to sanctity?

"My daughter, what will you do when I am gone?

Who will direct and protect you? Who will keep you in the paths of holiness?"

Elizabeth did not seem concerned.

"Dear Father, I shall have no need for protection. It is not you who will die, it is I."

Four days later, Elizabeth was stricken with a fever. As she lay on her wooden plank, her face shone with such radiance that crowds of people came to look and wonder. After twelve days had passed, Elizabeth asked that the doors be closed. She wanted to be alone with God and prepare herself for death. Master Conrad came and heard her confession. There was really nothing to confess, but she wept lest she might have forgotten something. She received the Sacred Host and lay lost in meditation.

Guda and Isentrude were allowed to come, and she smiled at them lovingly. "My beloved friends, my good and faithful companions."

And it is said she gave them her most priceless possession, the old patched cloak of Brother Francis, with which she had never parted.

When Master Conrad asked how he should dispose of her possessions, she answered, "I have no heirs but Jesus Christ."

Now the light about her head was so bright that those in the room had to turn away their eyes. Suddenly, Elizabeth began to sing.

"Did you hear the lovely song of the bird? I had to sing, too."

When she saw those about her weeping, she said softly, "Daughters of Jerusalem, weep not for me but for yourselves."

At midnight—it was November 16—she called on the Mother of God. Then she spoke again.

"The moment has come when Almighty God will call his friend to himself."

A moment later, she tried to lift her head.

"The moment has come . . . silence . . . silence . . ."

Then all at once the whole room was filled with the radiance of heaven. God had called to himself his faithful servant, the Princess Elizabeth of Hungary. She had never wanted anything but to do his will. Now he sent his troops of angels down to give her back her crown again, to exchange her old patched habit for a golden garment, and to place her among the shining ranks of saints.

12

THE FINAL CROWN

"SEE THE LITTLE ONE walk! That child has never before even stood on his feet!"

"Have you seen the crippled cobbler? He has thrown away his crutches and walks as well as you or I."

"Praise God, I can see again! I can see! I can see!"

The funeral was over. Elizabeth's body rested in a simple tomb in the chapel of her beloved hospital.

Crowds of people, many of whom had rejected her before, now milled about the door trying to get in and touch the stone under which she lay.

The very day after the funeral a Cistercian monk was suddenly cured of a forty-years' illness. After that, miracle after miracle occurred, some of them astounding, showing that Elizabeth had not forgotten the poor whom she had loved.

Master Conrad made note of everything that happened. Everyone was sure by now that, without question, Elizabeth was a saint. The crowds of sick and afflicted that continued to come to her tomb were so great that only a year later it was necessary to build a new church in place of the little chapel.

About the same time Master Conrad sent a careful record of the most important miracles to Pope Gregory, together with his own account of Elizabeth's life since he had known her and his belief in her sanctity. The Pope appointed a commission to study the facts and make an official report. In the year 1233 that report was completed and sent to Pope Gregory.

Meanwhile, however, Master Conrad had become involved in a feud between the Church and a sect of heretics against whom he had preached violently. He made many enemies, and one night, when he and a Franciscan brother were returning to Marburg, they were attacked. Both were killed. Master Conrad was buried in Marburg not far from the tomb of Elizabeth.

Although the documents with regard to Elizabeth's

life and the miracles after her death were already in the hands of the Pope, the matter was not taken up again until 1234. It was probably Henry and Conrad who hastened matters. Conrad is known to have visited Pope Gregory that summer. They were both convinced that their brother's wife, the little girl they had played with, was now a saint.

There were practical matters to attend to as well. The hospital built by Elizabeth in Marburg was turned over to a religious order. Conrad, who in particular had been greatly moved by Elizabeth's death, began to live a life of prayer and penance.

Pope Gregory appointed a new commission, consisting of a bishop and two abbots, who examined and approved the first documents and gathered more evidence from Guda, Isentrude, and others who had been with Elizabeth at Marburg. They also took testimony from well over a hundred witnesses who had been miraculously cured by visiting Elizabeth's tomb or merely by praying to her. Many of those cured were children, whose parents testified for them.

The testimony of Guda and Isentrude was very important because they had known Elizabeth better than anyone else, having played with her, prayed with her, and, in her last days, shared in her poverty and sufferings as well as in her good works. There wasn't much about Elizabeth that they didn't know.

It was Guda who testified about Elizabeth's childish love of God, her cleverness at inventing games that would give her a chance to enter the chapel, her small mortifications, and her patience under ill-treatment.

Both Guda and Isentrude recalled how Elizabeth had a secret place under the castle wall where she took care of the sick beggars. They told also about her life after her marriage and after Master Conrad came. "She would ride for forty miles over rough roads and then eat nothing but black bread soaked in water because of Master Conrad's orders", Guda remembered. They told about the hair shirts and other severe penances. They recalled, too, how many times God provided suitable clothes for Elizabeth when she had given away all her own.

There were so many little things to tell about Elizabeth, things that were not little in the sight of God. She loved to take part in all the ceremonies of the Church—to walk in the processions on Rogation days, to act as godmother for the babies of the poor, and to follow the Stations of the Cross on foot as the Franciscans had already begun to do.

Both of the girls testified to the seemingly cruel commands by which Master Conrad tried to break Elizabeth's will and test her fortitude. They also told of the many visions that she had. She seemed rarely to mention particular saints. It was Christ crucified who filled her mind and heart and drew her more and more closely to himself.

When all the facts were in order, the documents were signed by a large number of bishops, abbots, and other Church dignitaries, as well as by well-known knights and leading citizens of Marburg.

The great day came on Pentecost Sunday in the year 1235. The Papal Court was meeting in Perugia. With all the glorious pageantry with which the Church delights to honor those who have earned the highest places in heaven, Pope Gregory IX proclaimed Elizabeth a saint—Saint Elizabeth of Hungary. The great bells rang in jubilation, the huge congregation chanted the *Te Deum* in gratitude for a new saint in heaven, and the world began to pray to Saint Elizabeth.

Conrad, now known as Brother Conrad, on that same day made presents of decorated candles to all the clergy and ordinary wax candles to the others present. In the name of his own family and to honor Elizabeth, he also gave alms to thousands of poor people.

In May of the same year, 1235, the body of Elizabeth was moved from the hospital chapel to a great new church in Marburg, dedicated to her. How astonished the humble Elizabeth would have been to have seen the grandeur with which that ceremony was performed. Only a few years earlier, she had begged from door to door and had been turned away. She who had been obliged to seek shelter in an old shed rested now in a magnificent Gothic church richly furnished and adorned with stained glass windows depicting scenes from her life.

All the Thuringian royal family was there: Landgravine Sophie, who had always tried to be fair and just with Elizabeth; Landgrave Henry, now the head of the family; Conrad, a fine and noble knight; and the children.

What thoughts must have passed through the minds of those children! Not many people in this world have seen their own mothers glorified as saints. There was Hermann, fourteen, big and blond like his father, already showing himself a leader. There was Sophie, twelve, who had always clung to her mother so lovingly, and little Gertrude, now nine, who had been brought from the convent in Altenburg. Not much more than nine years before, Louis and Elizabeth had ridden out into the countryside and planned what would become of her, the child yet unborn, if he did not come back from the crusade.

Walter of Varila was there, too, with many memories. So were Guda and Isentrude, their hearts so full that they could not speak a word. They had always believed that Elizabeth was a saint. Many of the other knights of the Wartburg Castle, as well as vassals and old household servants, had also come for the ceremony.

"The emperor! The emperor!"

It was, indeed, the emperor himself, that same Frederick whom the Saracens had fed in the palace in Naples, that Frederick whom Louis had loved and served, that Frederick who had offered his crown to Elizabeth.

The emperor came barefoot and dressed in penitential robes, but he wore his golden crown. When the casket was opened, the whole church was fragrant with the delicate perfume from Elizabeth's body. The emperor stepped forward and placed his crown on Elizabeth's head.

"Since I could not crown her as empress in the world, I will at least crown her today immortal queen in the Kingdom of God."

And what of Elizabeth's children? They had just heard their mother glorified as a saint, they had seen the emperor place his crown upon her head, and now they walked out of the great church built in her honor into the common light of day. They would have to go back to their everyday lives and try, as well as they could, to conduct themselves worthily as the children of a saint.

Hermann assisted his uncle, Landgrave Henry, in the government of Thuringia and was involved in many political disputes, just as his father had been. He was married at an early age, but he died without children at the age of nineteen.

Sophie, the practical one, as her mother had called her, was married at fifteen to the Duke of Brabant. When Landgrave Henry, who was childless, died after a fall from his horse, she claimed the Thuringian throne for her own children. She carried on endless feuds, arguments, and battles, but she won out. The descendants of Louis and Elizabeth spread all over

Europe. Sophie turned out to be generous and pious and lived to the age of sixty.

Gertrude, the dedicated child who grew up in the Convent of Altenburg, was most nearly like her mother. She became a Premonstratensian nun, as her parents had expected, and devoted herself to the care of the poor and to other good works. At the age of twenty-one she was made abbess of her convent and remained abbess for forty-nine years. She built a beautiful Gothic church near the convent, very much like that of Saint Elizabeth in Marburg. Gertrude lived to the age of seventy and was considered so holy that she was beatified. Her cause was never completed, however, and she still remains Blessed Gertrude of Altenburg.

And what became of Guda and Isentrude? No one seems to have considered them important enough to record their lives after the death of Elizabeth. It is believed that both became nuns, but there is no certain trace of them at all. It seems rather a pity not to know what became of them, but God knows, and we may be sure that they received in heaven the reward of their faithful service.

Elizabeth was not the only saint in her family, by any means, but she was the greatest. Saint Hedwig, her mother's sister, was a very famous nun, although she did not enter a convent until after the death of her husband. The Sisters of Saint Hedwig were founded in her honor.

Saint Louis of Toulouse was a great-nephew of Elizabeth, grandson of her own brother, King Bela of Hungary. He died in 1297 when he was only twenty-three years old and was considered so holy that he was canonized almost immediately

Then there was the famous Saint Elizabeth of Portugal, a great-niece of Elizabeth of Hungary and known in Spanish-speaking countries as Saint Isabel. Like her aunt, she was a pious little girl, brought up very strictly. She, too, fasted, gave up amusements, performed penances, and was beset by court envy and jealousy. Like Elizabeth, she married early, but her husband was very unlike Louis. He led a wicked life and caused his wife much trouble. After his death, Elizabeth of Portugal retired to a convent of Poor Clares and joined the Third Order of the Franciscans. Thus, some of the spirit of Elizabeth of Hungary continued to appear in her descendants.

The church in Marburg became a place of pilgrimage for kings, bishops, lords and ladies, and just ordinary human beings bringing problems and petitions to the one who had never failed them. Many, many more miracles were recorded, and on feast days colorful processions and ceremonies were held to do honor to the saint. For centuries, one of the most famous shrines in Europe was that of Saint Elizabeth.

Saint Elizabeth of Hungary has usually been regarded as the most glorious saint produced by the Middle Ages. It was not only because of her penances and good deeds, which are, after all, characteristic of many saints. It was because, trained as she was in the feudal system and in spite of all opposition, she set herself against the medieval social pattern. She believed in the equality of man, and she shared all she had with the poor. She followed closely the teachings of Saint Francis of Assisi and became the patron saint of the Third Order.

The little four-year-old princess who rode to her destiny in a silver cradle and served God with all her heart for twenty years slept her eternal sleep with the earthly crown of an emperor on her head, but her radiant soul was crowned by God with a heavenly crown. And on November 17, which, in the calendar of saints, is now observed as her feast day, not only the Franciscan Order but the whole Catholic Church prays to Saint Elizabeth of Hungary

---

Enlighten, O merciful God, the hearts of thy faithful, and through the glorious prayers of blessed Elizabeth do thou make us despise worldly prosperity and ever be gladdened by that consolation which is of heaven.

Amen.

AUTHOR'S NOTE

In the case of Saint Elizabeth of Hungary, as in that of most medieval saints, a considerable body of legend has become interwoven with fact. Old records often contradict each other, and proper names vary in form and spelling according to the language of different countries. Saint Elizabeth's father, for example, is recorded sometimes as Andreas, sometimes as Andrew.

In preparing this life of Saint Elizabeth for young people, I have tried to concentrate on those stories and incidents most commonly agreed upon by reputable writers. In this respect I am particularly indebted to two excellent books in which the available data has been unusually well organized: *Saint Elizabeth,* by Elizabeth von Schmitt-Pauli (Holt, 1932), and *Saint Elizabeth of Hungary*, by Nesta de Robeck (Bruce, 1954), the latter being very well documented. In addition, I have naturally consulted a large number of references, including the Catholic Encyclopedia and many books on medieval customs, culture, and costumes; Hungarian and German history; and records of the crusades.

The main facts, dates, and incidents in *Saint Elizabeth's Three Crowns* are historically correct, and the proper names used are those most commonly used and recognized. I have given names to one or two shadowy characters, invented necessary dialogue, and expanded certain incidents in order to give a better idea of the kind of life Elizabeth lived in the Wartburg Castle.